MELODY OF MANA

✦ BOOK 5 ✦

MELODY OF MANA

✦ BOOK 5 ✦

WANDERING AGENT

Podium

Cover design by Yanhong Lu

ISBN: 978-1-0394-4392-1

Published in 2024 by Podium Publishing
www.podiumaudio.com

MELODY OF MANA

✦ BOOK 5 ✦

Mother wanted to spend an afternoon together before I got up to anything else. Even though there was work to be done back at the lab, I really had no reason to refuse her. We'd proven our concept, and the safety checks were ongoing. I got a brief note from Dras—who had stayed behind to finish his core improvement and keep training—informing me that we'd all be off for about a week.

In my previous world, we might have done a number of things. Sadly, many of those things were not really viable here. For instance, shopping wasn't something that was viewed as a common activity for ladies to engage in for fun at our social level. Clothing was incredibly expensive, and even though my family was now quite well-off, my wardrobe could still easily be described as . . . anemic. That wasn't odd, as most people only had a few outfits, and seldom bought more. As for more common goods, most of those were delivered to us by merchants now, so going to the market would be seen as unusual as well.

Most beauty treatments were done at home. It wasn't the same social experience as on Earth, sadly. Since the wealthy had staff, beauty treatments were almost always done in private, and were quite time consuming. Public baths were starting to catch on in a few places and served as something of a full spa, but Mother had been raised in a small village and they made her uncomfortable.

There were a number of theaters and performances that we could go to. However, Mother and I disagreed on what we liked to watch, and it wasn't really conducive to chatting as an activity. The most common shows were big circus-type exhibitions, stage plays, or concerts of various genres. I did have to admit that some of the plays were pretty good, even if a bit raunchy at times.

The most common social activity for women of every order was handcrafts. There was always more work that needed doing, or small things that could be repaired or improved with decoration. I hated handcrafts to a certain extent, but they weren't without purpose, and if it made Mom happy I could grit my teeth for a while. I'd learned the most common ones, and even if I was below average, I could fake it well enough for most of them.

I did not expect my mother to have gotten into lace while I was away, but apparently she had. She'd taken to it like a fish to water and started decorating a large number of things around the house—something I'd missed the night before. Lacework was time consuming, painfully difficult, was only really suited to making things look fancy, and required extremely fine thread for her patterns.

That last part was where I came in. I had no intention of following her into this new hobby, but more than any other of her womanly arts, I'd kept up with spinning. Mainly because I could do it anywhere and the tools were easy to keep nearby, the hobby not requiring much space or setup. This world was still using drop spindles.

"So, tell me about this man you've met," she began as soon as we'd gotten started.

"There's not really much to tell, Mother," I responded.

"Oh? How did you meet?"

"Our group hired him to join us in our work. A lot of people died and we needed help." That stopped her in her tracks.

"I . . . didn't hear about that."

"Well, Mother, we lost about two-thirds of our people before we even got to the Elven lands," I explained.

"Are you okay?" Her voice shook with concern.

"I'm fine. I can't say I really knew them, and it wasn't like we . . ." It was hard to explain, even if I kept to the current knowledge available to the public about what we were doing. "There was a monster, a big one."

"Like the one your father fought?" she said, referring to the giant lizard from when I was a child. "I remember the injuries, and how you were after seeing those men."

"It was a lot worse than that. We were prepared—at least we thought we were—but not for some of the things that live in the seas. Even once we made landfall, there were more of them, more beasts and creatures.

The leader of our team died too. A big rock fell and crushed him like paste right in front of me." I'd stopped spinning at some point. As I sat there looking at the work, I felt a pair of arms wrap around me.

"Are you okay?" she asked again, holding me gently.

My mother had almost always been harsh and demanding, and more than a little irritating at times, but still, she tried to do her best to help me. Sure, we disagreed on a lot of things—really, a lot of things—and lived very different lives, but she still taught me the things she really thought I needed, and got angry when I pushed back against what she viewed as important lessons.

"I'm fine. Even if I'd gotten hurt, I could have just healed myself," I said, pouting.

"That's not what I mean, and you know it. You're strong, Alana, and you've seen and done things I know I never will, but you're still only human."

"I'm . . ." Was I fine, though? I could keep saying it, but was it true? "It seems like no matter where I go, there's always something horrible there. People around me are always getting hurt or dying. Am I cursed or something?"

"You're not cursed, Alana. No more than anyone else of this age. We've all lost people—a lot of them in the last few years—to the famine, the wars, and all of that. You do have the ability to find trouble though, and, despite how much I beg you not to, you always seem to run straight at it."

I had to think on that for a bit. I could have stayed at the orphanage as a child. I could have not gone down into the Undercity with Dras and the others, or not taken combat magic even though people told me it would be a mess. I could have taken a nice, quiet job anywhere, and made lots of money with my magic. I could even have done as Mother seemed to want and settle down, having a few kids and a nice, quiet family life. I could have. . . but I also couldn't.

"I don't want trouble, Mother, I want to be out there. I want—need—to be somewhere, seeing the edges of the world and learning about the newest and greatest things. I need freedom too. Being tied down to one place just isn't for me."

"And this man, will he help you with that?" she asked.

"How . . . how did you take me through an entire conversation about feelings only to come right back around to the boy-talk?" I'd just run through about five emotions and back.

"It's a skill you'll learn when you have children." She narrowed her eyes. "*If* you have children." That was a low blow in her book. "You didn't answer my question though. Will he?"

I had to think about that for a few minutes. "Don't know. But I know he'll keep me safe."

"Good enough, I suppose. I don't really need to know anything else then," she said.

My head was still spinning from that roller coaster of a conversation, but I did feel better. We spent the rest of the day working on our chosen tasks. Mom asked about other things, how people were, and if they were doing well. Then she told me about some of the things going on back home while I'd been away.

One of our former maids, a nice girl named Suzanne, was slated to marry Charles, of all people. Mom was glad she'd found someone, as the girl had been a bit messed up. Apparently, she'd been a slave back before Ermath fell and had some very odd views of the world. Having a new husband meant that she'd no longer be working for us, but Mom was happy regardless. I was just happy Charles finally found someone, as he was an oddball too.

She also told me that my friend Pinea, the queen of all partiers, had recently been seen often in the presence of a man named Alowen. He was recently out of the military and had taken up a high position in the city's guard. I'd have to ask Pinea about it sometime in the future.

We finished up late that afternoon when the things I'd ordered arrived. I had mice and tools to unpack and set up—something Mother was completely uninterested in aiding me with. She knew it was for my practice, but outright hated the sight of mice. They'd been carriers of disease and a blight upon food for most of her life, so keeping them around was quite against her nature. But I imagined she'd approve if she knew I planned to kill them later.

I also received a letter from Ulanion later in the day, asking to see me. I recognized the meeting place as one of the more pleasant eateries in the city, but the time . . . Why in the world would he possibly need to meet that early in the morning? I shrugged and replied with my confirmation, not thinking too much about it. Perhaps he had a weird schedule.

CHAPTER 2

✦

BREAKFAST AT DAWN

Days passed, and while I still had a few things to do, it felt like a vacation. I worked on my spells in the afternoon and spent time with my family whenever possible. I even managed to borrow a maid from my mother to help me get ready the morning of my meeting with Ulanion.

I rose slowly as the girl woke me. There were no alarm clocks here, but there were still plenty of ways to measure time, and there was always someone awake at the house. As I shuffled over to the small dresser, she spoke.

"Don't worry, Miss Alana. I'll have you right ready for your date."

I was instantly awake. A date? No, no this was way too early. It was . . . breakfast time. I cursed internally, bemoaning how often I had neglected the common customs of this world. I'd been on practically zero actual dates over the years, and had totally forgotten. Here they liked to go on dates at the start of the day.

"I . . . thank you," I attempted to say. It was too late. I couldn't back out now without massive repercussions.

If only I'd thought this through. He wanted to go to one of the nicer restaurants in town and probably asked around for good places. Any other girl, any *normal* human girl in this country would have understood in a heartbeat, but no, I had to have a whole lifetime of non-matching social information buzzing around in my head.

The maid was happy, seemingly thinking that my mood—for I was in quite a mood—was just nerves. I also had to admit that she was very good at her job. I knew how to do my hair and makeup, and get dressed, but there was really no substitute for having professional help. By the time she finished, I looked excellent. I was glad choosing my clothes wasn't an issue, as I had rather few, and even fewer that would be proper for this date.

"You look perfect; he'll be thrilled," she declared as I finally stood before the mirror in my room.

"Thank you, you're really good at this," I said. The girl smiled and winked before going to get the carriage.

The air around the restaurant was quiet and subdued. Magical, colored lights shone from behind hidden corners and curtains. The lighting was indirect, warming the room, but not bright enough to disturb any of the patrons. The tables were similarly arrayed with bright colors and fresh flowers, the whole place evoked the image of a fresh, spring day at dawn.

Ulanion was waiting for me near the entrance. He wore a lovely outfit in cool blues based on military garb. That was the standard dress, particularly since he was in some capacity working for the army. It looked magnificent on him.

He raised an eyebrow as I looked him over. "Something wrong?" he asked.

"Where in the world did you get those?" I responded, indicating his outfit.

"Ah, a particular tailor. Lovely man. I must admit that I've never before seen a bard who used magic to mold and create in that medium." He offered his hand as the waiter approached to lead us to our table.

We engaged in a bit of small talk, catching up for a bit until our food arrived. Orders hadn't been taken, but rather the dishes were based on what ingredients were freshest. It was a nice meal consisting of fresh fruit and things like porridge.

"I wasn't sure you would come," he finally said. "I'm not quite familiar with how humans do things, so I was a bit worried that I might have made some faux pas."

"Why would you think you'd messed things up?"

"Well, it had been some time since we last spoke, when I told you . . ." he started, "and I know you do things . . . quite differently."

"To be honest, I didn't realize until this morning that you were asking me out," I admitted.

"Really?" He looked outright floored by that. "But . . . isn't this standard practice for humans?"

"It is. Thing is, I haven't been on all that many dates, particularly not ones so formal." He still looked stunned. "So, this isn't how things are done in Atali? How do your people date or court or whatever?"

"Well, it depends. Typically, you ask someone if they'd like to join you at a festival. There's music and dancing, games and things like that. They come often enough, and if you both have fun, well, you go again. That continues until the couple decides to make things permanent." He sighed. "It's not so formal, and not so . . . well, early."

I nodded. "Honestly, the early morning thing has always thrown me too. I get why, but it's just a lot right after waking up. I have to admit, going to a festival does sound more fun."

"I haven't heard of any upcoming, but if you'd like to?" He tilted his head. "Sadly, they're very rare. The normal time for gatherings and celebrations is winter, when nobody has anything to do. There are some in summer, but spring is busy for most people. Between making sure the fields are right and all the work around that, and the administration of it all, everyone is just busy." His face fell, seemingly in understanding. "But if you find something you think looks fun . . ." At that he perked right back up.

"I'll be sure to invite you," he declared.

"Please do." I still wasn't completely sure if this would go anywhere, but he was nice, and I did like him.

A small bell rang lightly, drawing everyone's attention to a small man who stood to the side. "Esteemed guests, the sun will be rising shortly. For those who wish to watch the spectacle, we have a viewing platform just upstairs."

We looked at each other and shrugged, then went to see what all the hype was about. The platform was much the same as the eatery below, but lacking seats. There was plenty of room for everyone who wanted to stand near their partner and look at the brightening east.

I hadn't watched too many sunrises before. I really preferred the stars in the night sky. Though, as the first rays pierced the horizon, I understood. The morning sky was so bright and clear in this world, so unmarred by pollution or cityscapes that it was something I could watch again and again.

Pink and gold exploded outward as the sun crested, bright light flowing onto the world. Buildings that had looked drab from the street now shone brightly. The fields and farms around lit up green as the wave of light crept across. Something about the crisp air made it all seem far brighter and more vibrant.

"How beautiful," I said idly.

"Indeed," Ulanion agreed. But out of the corner of my eye, I noticed he wasn't looking at the dawn.

CHAPTER 3

✦

NEW MEETINGS
AND OLD FRIENDS

I sat at a small table in my room, looking at the poor, dead mouse. It had worked, sort of. I had managed to kill it with a spell. Sadly, it had not been an easy death on the poor little creature, which had struggled and fought until its body gave out.

It wasn't the first; there were a few now. My idea to make a spell that replicated the feeling of drowning was functional. It was also horrid to watch.

The worst part was that in this particular case I'd been trying to make my magic work without singing, or what I felt was a clear performance—no dancing or the like. I'd tried a few things with varying results. Poetry was hit-and-miss. My working theory was that it had to be performed, and just reading it wasn't enough. Perhaps if I made it up as I went. Acting was also hit-or-miss and was what I'd used in this case. The trick there was that it had to be clearly acting, not something that might be mistaken for reality.

I had literally killed this poor creature with my bad acting. There were so many jokes there, but I couldn't bear getting into them. They rang a bit sour, as I didn't much like the idea of torturing small animals, only using them as a necessity.

I'd had about a week of working from home, but tomorrow I'd have to go back to the lab and start again with whatever we were doing. I wasn't sure how that would go, being that my ostensible manager was now dead, and his replacement, if there was one, hadn't yet been introduced to us. Though if anyone tried to give me that job, I might just quit.

There were a number of letters from Ulanion on my desk beside the paperwork. We wrote just about every day since our breakfast, an alternative to phone conversations. He was too busy for any real dates at the moment—and I would soon be busy too—but this was not bad. It was . . . calmer, and less stressful than I'd been expecting.

I put him out of my mind and went to bed. There would be much to do, a lot of which couldn't be handled via anything but conversation in person.

I rose with the sun the next morning and got my stuff together. Since my work was top secret and was absolutely never allowed to be taken home, my things mostly consisted of personal effects. It was interesting how Durin's people ran things. It was all controlled, much more like how a modern military might run than I'd expected. I knew that he'd read some of Ristolian's works, but I had to wonder if those covered information control and its importance in war and governance, or if that was common before and I'd just never seen it.

The office was the same as it had always been—armed guards, lots of searches and scans on your way in, essentially the works. After my time away it seemed very personal, but none of the procedures had changed much. Shortly enough, I was through and down to the lower levels where the real work happened.

When I got to the team workshop, I found Dras and Selene already there, looking tired as the examined the place.

"Anything new?" I asked.

"Yeah, look at our supplies," Selene responded.

It was impressive. There were stacks of raw materials, metals marked with their alloy description, mana-conductive wood, magical creature body parts, and even a small box of gems. The last were only useful in a few specialty magic tools, but those could cost a fortune to make.

"Someone's got a new project for us. Lots of gates based on that pile," I commented.

"Well, you'll be finding out soon enough, I believe," a voice interrupted.

I turned to see a prim-looking young man with spectacles. I'd seen him a few times here and there but couldn't quite place him. He certainly had authorization to be here, based on the fact that the guards in the hall hadn't taken him apart, but I didn't know him personally.

"Excuse me, but I don't believe we've met," Selene observed.

"Ah, forgive me. I'm one of the archmage's apprentices. My name is Jason." He made a little bow. "It's a shame that I've not had the chance to meet with one of my seniors as well." He nodded to me.

Archmage wasn't an official moniker, but rather a broad descriptor. It wasn't an "If you do x and then y, then you become an archmage" situation. Rather, it was just a word used for incredibly powerful spellcasters. Most would certainly have managed to get their core to its third and final stage, sure, and most could take on dozens of lesser casters, but there wasn't a hard-and-fast rule. There was, however, only one person here who could take that title.

"A pleasure to meet you, Jason, but I haven't been trained by Mystien in many years," I said, nodding back.

"Perhaps, but I can tell by the way he pays attention to your work that he still values you. At any rate, I'm not here for a purely social call, rather to inform you that our collective boss would like a word, and a meeting with all of you."

"Nice to meet you. I'm Dras. I specialize primarily in fire magic," Dras interrupted, taking the initiative.

"Selene. My focus is a bit more broad, but if anything, I'm here because I excel in magical items," Selene said and waved with a small smile.

"And I'm Alana, support magic and item specialist. I'm not quite as good at making new things as Selene here, but I do better at finding issues and fixing them."

"Well met, everyone, shall we?" He motioned to the hall.

As we headed up, we chatted lightly. Jason had been recruited by Mystien during the war, and had served with him throughout. He was a wizard, and his specialty was of course water. I knew that my old teacher had a number of students that he'd taken in, but we'd drifted apart, at least to an extent.

"Come in," the old man called at our knock.

Mystien's office was a Spartan affair. There were shelves packed with books, a desk piled high with research notes and paperwork, and a very comfortable-looking chair for the man himself, but not much else. It almost reminded me of his house back in the village—nice, but more plain than most rich folk's residences.

As for the man himself, it struck me hard how much he'd aged. Sure, he'd been old when I met him, but seeing him in this place really made me think about how many years had gone by. He was looking more like the wizened old mage you'd see on the cover of a fantasy book back on Earth and less like the spry, hard-worn elder I'd known in my childhood.

"Something wrong?" he asked upon seeing my face.

"Sorry, just been thinking a lot today. I realized how much you've changed since we first met."

My remark got a scoff from the old wizard. "You're one to talk. Ah, but let's reminisce another time—we've business to discuss." He cleared his throat and looked us over. "I'm glad you've all met Jason, and I do hope you'll get along. He'll be joining you for some much-needed support. With the loss of your previous leader, and the outright destruction of the majority of the portal creation teams, we need badly to get to rebuilding."

"So . . . is Jason our new supervisor?" Selene asked.

"Not in the same way. Jason is skilled at administrative work and war magic, and will be aiding you with that, but you four will all be reporting directly to me for the time being. We've got a number of things that need doing now, particularly since we've proven the concept of portals as viable."

Papers were passed out, outlining a few short-term goals. We needed to get enough support staff who could get portals up and running, as well as standardize portal control and build layouts. The emperor also wanted to get our first working pair out as soon as possible. There was a note that he'd already concluded plans for installing the first pair.

"We've got our first order in already?" I asked. That was fast by any metric.

"Yes, Emperor Durin is quite eager to get some out into the world," Jason answered.

"Indeed," Mystien agreed. "Dras here will go back to the improvement of his core. The stone used for such has been released to us, and is in a secure place. I'll be taking you there after this meeting. As for you two." He looked at Selene and myself. "I'd like you to see if you can come up with a way to transport a portal, assembled or not, through another. If it isn't possible, that's fine, but our hope is that it will be, as that will simplify things greatly. Once you've done that, we'll need one to test, and then ship out. You two will be on that project for the time being."

We split to go about our assigned tasks. Discussion of important projects wasn't allowed outside of rooms, so I had time to think. I realized that while I'd been told we had a place, we hadn't been told where. A quick scan of the papers revealed that it wasn't written there either. That was no mistake—we wouldn't be told until we needed to be.

CHAPTER 4

✦

TOWARD CONVERGENCE

Making a gate that could be taken through another was a challenge, but not an insurmountable one. There needed to be a way to keep the item as one, while still being able to take it apart or down. We spent several days bouncing ideas back and forth to little effect.

The issue was that magical items really, really did not like being added to or broken down after they were made. In many cases it was known that would destroy the item completely. Even things like the city wards, were done in a simplistic method. A power output and on/off control was put somewhere, and then the energy was moved over in an on/off manner. That was it. I'd never personally gotten a close look at the city wards, as they were need-to-know, but I'd wager they were a disaster of overlapping and aggregated items.

We could have possibly scaled them down significantly, but Jason didn't like that—the point was for them to be large. A letter from Mystien himself said that we could if no other method would work, but we were to investigate all other avenues first.

"None of these are working," I groaned.

"Hmm, what if we connected all the pieces through that thing you used, the—" Jason hesitated. Up until recently, the communications had been absolutely top secret, but after a moment he remembered. "Right, right, the communications things. Can we use those? Maybe add them so that the parts are all connected?"

I had to take a moment to think about that one. "Hmm, I don't think that would work. If they're not all together at some point, then we might have some real issues if the portal tries to activate. It's just not gonna be clean."

We played with the idea of having the portal appear in the air, and even ran a trial. The result was a disastrous failure. Without being able to connect to a frame, the portal began distorting space around it in dangerous ways, much like my first couple of attempts with a spell version, though this faded quicker. It made the team step back very carefully and put that idea down, and also led to some changes in protocol.

"How do you think that mage, Ristolian, did it?" Jason asked.

It wasn't the first time I'd considered that question.

"I think he knew how to teleport. Or maybe he just flew them into place. Records on that guy are scarce, but he was a known powerhouse when he was active. There are still accounts of some of his exploits in the magical schools. Our first dean even knew of him, though not about this." I thought for a moment. "Well, if he did know about teleportation, he kept it hidden—but he'd have been able to act against the emperor if he did."

Selene sighed and reached for a little paper fan. The room wasn't hot or anything, but she'd taken to playing with it to help her think—much to our irritation. She snapped the thing open again with a *crack* and froze.

"Got something?" I asked.

"Yeah. Maybe I do."

The next week was spent designing and then making a frankly ugly construction of folding metal. Joints had to be constructed with care, so they would bend but not break. It wasn't our loveliest work, and certainly still in the prototype stage without any real spells in it, but we could use test runes to check if it all connected. The first few had been tiny models that shifted this way and that before finally locking into a circular formation. Once opened, they needed new pieces to keep them in shape for activation, but that was only a minor setback.

With magic, we could design, then create, a trial version within hours. The wizards in our group were particularly skilled at molding the pieces with little more than a blueprint and their minds. I could use an array of magically powered tools to achieve a similar result, but they were much better at this than me.

Instead, I added a few extra safety measures. If the portal couldn't achieve the right shape, or if any part of the circuit broke, the whole thing would shut off. It was a small addition, but I wanted to be sure that if something did break, it wouldn't happen in a way that killed anyone. I also made sure to check on that little spatial distortion we'd made. Luckily, it had dispersed, leaving no traces. But I still checked daily.

"So this is it?" Mystien asked when he came to see our prototype.

"Yeah. It's not pretty, but it should work," Jason answered.

"It may just be the ugliest item I've ever seen." The old man gave it a critical eye. "But does it work?"

"We'll be ready to test it tomorrow. We were thinking that we'd take it through a gate somewhere. Of course we need permission for that," I said, leaning over.

"You'll have it. Don't need any accidents." Mystien was nothing if not pragmatic. "If it works as desired, we'll need a pair, preferably nicer ones, as soon as possible."

"What's the rush?" Dras asked.

"We've gotten approval and you'll be off to install it as soon as possible. The emperor wants to start the expansion process right away. Ah, but the new hub will be in the capital, not here or in the fortress," he answered.

That was exciting. I'd never been there, and would probably have to go at some point, if only for the installation.

Somewhere else, a large caravan was trudging along. The merchants that accompanied them had fish, dried and salted. They moved these first, trading them for oil and dried fruit. At one point they picked up a load of fine cloth, only for it to be transferred a few cities further upon their way.

They weren't out to make money. Several of the people here were, of course, but that wasn't the main goal. In a number of their trades, they actually took losses. This was unfortunate, but as long as they were trading, it was fine.

There weren't many magic users on board, at least to untrained eyes. A handful of auras were tightly suppressed, mostly from physical types. Similarly, those who looked closely would realize that most of these men, even the ones without any magic at all, were in better shape than your standard caravan trader, loaded with lean muscle.

Though nobody would think that about the driver of the third cart. He was an older man with wrinkles formed around his long face, slitted eyes, and a look that filled others with mistrust and fear. He had the look of a viper on the hunt. One not to be denied.

It would be quite the trip, and the man looked most displeased to make it. After all, the city of Linden was far from the frozen north. What was one to do when their prince needed results though, other than go himself?

CHAPTER 5

✦

THE GRID

The trip to the capital was short. I still thought of my own home city of Lithere as the capital in a lot of regards, but within the Empire of Shadows, that simply wasn't the case. Instead, it was the old Ermathi capital in the city of Ermath—wholly unimaginative, but things were like that sometimes.

The portal connection made what would have been a weeks-long trip into a short afternoon jaunt, but still we ended up outside the city proper. Sad to say, the capital did not live up to my expectations. It was ugly. There were clear signs of renovation, but the primary architecture of the city was brutalist and plain. Any decorations were all new additions and hadn't yet spread to every corner.

Lithere, on the other hand, was a city of layers. There were towers, homes, and businesses, all in various shapes and colors. Ermath was a city that looked like it had been built by a military hand. The buildings were boxy and uniform. There was no art, no variety in materials, no color on the buildings.

"I hate it," I said as we approached.

"It really isn't much to look at, is it?" Dras asked.

"Dras, it's in a grid pattern. You can see the lines. I bet they even leveled the land before they built here. Aside from the newer stuff, it's just ghastly."

"The Ermathi were always under a military dictatorship, but I never imagined it was this bad," Selene added.

As I looked on, I began to notice that all the surrounding fields and lands were almost the same, laid out in perfectly regular plots, all with the same basic structures. It was like the medieval version of a suburban hellscape—if it had been run by the most boring bureaucrats to ever live.

We made it through the gate with ease, as we were all clearly there on official government business, and things brightened somewhat. A few buildings did have murals on them, decorated signs hung here and there, and were clearly newer in construction. It was still brutal, but you could see some signs of hope in the citizens.

We slowly made our way to a building that was clearly new and appeared to be purposefully built just for this project. With magic, construction could go fast, but this was burning along at an insane pace. The building itself was clearly militarized, but also strangely welcoming. Around all the security structures, there were clear places for people. Benches stood outside, and if I wasn't mistaken, a few buildings were being renovated into something like a tavern.

We were dropped off at the main entrance and greeted by a man in a decorated black tunic. That was standard for government workers on the job—not an official uniform, but trying to fit with the country's whole aesthetic of evil overlord.

"Greetings, greetings welcome. Ah, Jason, is that you?" the man said, his arms wide.

"Hey there, Ron. Been a while, hasn't it?" Our newest member embraced the man warmly. "Ah, let me introduce my team. This is Selene, Dras, and Alana. Everyone, this is Ron, former military and the soon-to-be overseer of this new hub."

"How public is this going to be?" I asked after we made it through the first few sets of warded doors.

"The building giving you ideas, huh? For the near future, not at all. It will be a military installation, though we are trying to make it nice. If things proceed well and we can establish it, in the next decade or two your work will be made public, and it will be open to a limited extent." Ron didn't elaborate on what we were doing—none of us did—but that declaration got more than one pair of raised eyebrows.

"Sincerely?" Dras voiced.

"For the moment, this project is needed to secure and grow the empire, but surely you can see the benefit for civilians as well?" We followed him along a path.

"I think it's a wonderful idea, but it will change a lot of things," I pointed out.

We were finally led to the innermost room. The doors were massive, and nobody could miss the magic around the whole place. They could talk all they wanted about this building being for the people one day, but for now, this place was military, and a massive liability if things went wrong.

But as we entered, I could see the potential. The walls were blank, but the whole structure reminded me of something like a subway station. There was a central area, ostensibly for control around a concourse for people to go to portals not yet installed.

It would take a day to install the first gate. Most of that time would be spent dealing with the mess of importing and setting up the wards. Putting the gate in place was a rather simple action by comparison, but there was so much that had to be done around it that it was going to be a chore.

After an hour or two of discussion on what we'd need for the next day and when we'd start, we were taken to a nearby barracks. It was hard to tell one building here from another, but there were numbers, and the streets were laid out in a grid that followed a simple system.

Selene would be spending the night in the room beside mine. Dras was down the hall.

"All right," I declared after seeing that the small case I'd brought was in place. "I'm going out."

"Out where?" Selene asked, poking her head out of her own room.

"To a tavern. We're in a city, and cities have taverns. I want to see more of this place, because it's been pretty droll so far."

She nodded along. "Not what we're really here for, but okay. Want company?"

"Certainly. Let's see what we can find."

Dras stayed behind. Mostly because we didn't invite him. We were both full casters, and more than dangerous enough to take on almost anyone who would cause trouble for us. I also liked to think I had a pretty good handle on how to deal with city life after spending several years working in a tavern, but there were some issues.

"Okay," I groaned after a solid ten minutes of looking and still finding no signs of use. "How is this place even organized?"

"Maybe ask someone?" Selene shrugged. It wasn't her worst idea ever.

There were a few locals out on the street, even as the daylight began to dim.

"Excuse me, sir," I said, stopping a man who looked like he knew his way around. "I don't suppose you could recommend a tavern around here?"

"Um . . . one of the old drinking halls? Or one of the newer places?" he asked with a slight accent.

"Let's go with a newer one," I said, getting a nod from my companion.

"Most of those are over near the barracks. Abe's is pretty good." He gave us a weird address, something like +E-15.

We located a map and discovered the city was essentially a giant grid with the palace sitting in the dead center labeled A0. From there, letters indicated longitude labeled with a + symbol for east and a - for west. And numbers indicated latitude with negatives for north and positives for south. Therefore, the bar was slightly north and quite west of the palace. Incidentally, the new hub was at +G-18, not far from our destination. I'd been told that things could get a bit wonky with some of the new buildings but this was fortunately an easy place to find.

Selene was content to let me lead. Most of the buildings were quiet, but as we drew near our destination, I finally began to see signs of a nightlife. Here and there, obvious changes had been made to buildings; walls opened, and more decorations were visible on the formerly droll structures.

Abe's had a big sign out front and warm lights along the side. Though there was no loud ruckus, I could hear a slight strumming coming from within. Not one to be thrown by whatever weirdness was going on, I made my way to the door.

CHAPTER 6

◆

CULTURE SHOCK

The tavern was strikingly quiet. There were a few conversations going on, and someone played music in the background, but it was not the kind of wild taverns I was used to. The noise level reminded me of a high-end sort of place, but the decor and clients didn't match that either. Everyone was just . . . quiet.

I looked around, feeling a bit odd. I knew taverns. I'd lived in and worked in taverns for much of my youth. This place was strange. A few people gave me a passing look as I entered, but that lasted only a minute before they went back to their drinks and hushed talking. I didn't even get many guys checking me out, which was odd. I liked to think I was above average, and even more homely girls would get looked at when they entered one of these places.

My face must have betrayed my consternation, because the barman chuckled as I approached.

"First time in the city?" he asked.

"Yeah, I'm from further west, over near Lithere," I said as Selene came over to join me. Even she seemed surprised by the atmosphere.

"You've got the look of it. Always get a new crop when the soldiers rotate out, and they always have the same look you do," he explained.

"So, what's with . . ." I swept my arm out, gesturing around the room.

"Oh, that old *bastard* . . ." the barman started to say. At that word, someone else nearby spit to the side. "Oi, don't spit on my floor."

"Sorry, Abe," the man said, putting one hand up to the barman placatingly.

"Right then," Abe the barman, and I supposed the owner, continued. "That old bastard who used to rule this place, and most of his predecessors, hated things like art and music, and all the good things in life. Unless it was for the military, they tamped it down like a dying fire. Now, we've come a long way in these last few years, but most folk are still trying to get used to how Emperor Durin runs things."

I couldn't help but notice that several people raised glasses at his name, giving a quiet toast. I knew that he was liked by a lot of folk, particularly common folk, and there had been one boy who absolutely fanboyed over my father back in school, but this was extreme.

Selene looked a bit confused too. "How bad was it?" she inquired.

"Well, the really rich had more than you'd believe, and they could get things like music and art, all dedicated to combat of course. They could also do much as they pleased, treating everyone like slaves, *particularly* the slaves. It was . . . dark, though at the time nobody really knew how bad. Suppose if you live without any beauty to speak of, then anything seems bright." Abe smiled and got our order for drinks—a pair of ciders.

"I'm sorry to hear that," I said. "But it's better now?"

"Oh, loads and loads. So what brings you two to town then?" he asked.

"We just got done with an expedition for the government out on the Elven continent. Came to give some presentations on the flora and fauna there. And trade our goods, of course." I gave him the standard line, which wasn't technically a lie. We would spend a few minutes talking to a small crowd about some of our experiences, and ask questions tomorrow afternoon, after the real work was done.

"Well how about that! Right explorers, huh? Making our emperor proud?" Abe was a nice guy, jovial. Though I heard one man scoff at the mention of the Elven lands.

"I don't know if he was proud, but he certainly seemed happy enough last I saw him. Kind words and all." I could have smacked Selene as she spoke. She was giving away far too much.

"You've *spoken* to him?" Abe looked downright stunned, and several of those nearby leaned in to listen.

"Our expedition was at his behest, and we lost a lot of people. He came by to see the survivors after we returned," I added quickly, hoping that I could keep my partner from saying anything else.

This got a series of nods from people nearby. One man even commented, "Of course, that's what a decent leader would do."

I did not want to tell these people that we knew him, or had any real connection. I really didn't want them to know that my family and mentor were high up in the military. Based on the few former Ermathi citizens I knew, they all seemed fanatical about Durin. It was almost to the level of being creepy.

Selene seemed to get the message after that and shut up. I wasn't worried that she'd spill any state secrets, but more that she might say something to get us mobbed with people interested in our leader.

"So, if you're from out west, do you know any good songs? Lots of the soldiers passing through had some they liked to sing, and I think Ellen there is about to finish up for a bit," Abe asked, indicating the minstrel strumming the harp in the corner. I bet it was easy to get a slightly sloshed soldier to sing here, if only to break up the solemnness of the surroundings.

I chuckled. "One or two, yeah. Don't suppose I could use the harp?"

The instrument in question in fact belonged to Abe himself. The current performer, Ellen, was somehow related to the owner and looked a bit irked at giving it up. That all ended when I began to play.

I hardly kept up with all of my instruments, but I'd still been trained on them, and drilled well. I launched into a song about the pleasant darkness of the night, something I felt would go down well here. As I did, I began to weave an illusion across the ceiling.

Lucien had loved to weave the stars and sky above the patrons of his bar, and while I might not have quite his faculty with that particular illusion, it was still one of my specialties. As I wove the words and chords, I formed the images, spreading across the beams and ceiling. A few people in the crowd gasped as the stars and moon bloomed to life, bathing the onlookers with their soft light.

I didn't go on for too long. Not only was it bad to show off, but I wasn't working, just having a bit of fun.

"Y-you're a caster?" Abe asked as I returned to my seat. "Both of you?" He looked a little scared.

"Don't worry," I said, trying to calm him. "We're both in the service of Emperor Durin, and neither of us came here to cause any harm. It is the duty of the strong to protect the weak," I added in one of the pieces of propaganda that had been drilled into us in school.

I could tell that something about casters or magic users in general had frightened. No matter how much things might have changed in the years since the Empire of Shadows had taken over, there was still a bit of fear around the subject.

"Of course, sorry. That was beautiful. Why don't you have your drinks on the house tonight?" He recovered nicely.

We thanked him, and after finishing up our beverages, decided it was about time to head home. I was happy to see that Selene had the same thought as I did, and hid a couple coins under the glass before leaving. He may have offered the drinks to be free, but we both knew we were held to a standard, and paying was what we were expected to do. It wasn't like either of us were hurting for cash either.

The next morning's installation was, frankly, boring. It was a by-the-book thing that we needed to supervise because we were the go-to people on this, but it wasn't interesting. The spells had been gone over until they were just routine, so getting it done was no issue.

We gave our talk to a few scholars. I described the Hurricane Whale and its use of potent weather magic, along with what I could understand of its abilities. Being that I was a weather magic user, there weren't many considered more qualified, even if I still didn't really understand the details of it. The given reason for that talk was to tell them about the dangers without spilling secrets.

Dras stayed behind for now, at least until we got the other gate installed. Selene and I would be going onward to our installation point—a city called Linden. We'd be taking the gate network most of the way there but would have to travel a couple of weeks by carriage.

That afternoon, we decided to walk back to our temporary accommodations, and as we did, I saw something that was strikingly odd, and a bit terrifying.

There was a crowd, a large one, and a slightly buzzing, nearly angry atmosphere. They'd gathered in one of the squares along a larger road. At the back, looking new, were gallows.

We arrived just after the announcement of the crimes, as several men were brought up. It struck me that they all looked old, and rather larger than one might expect of hardened criminals.

Executions happened under Durin's rule—not many, but they did happen. The odd thing was that this was public. Public executions were very, very rare, almost vanishingly so. Victims, or their families in the case of murders, might be allowed to witness the end of a criminal, but allowing it to be seen by all was only done in the cases of truly heinous crimes, or those where a loud message needed to be sent.

"What did they do?" Dras whispered to a man nearby. "Sorry, I missed the announcement," he explained.

"Bankers," the man replied, looking disgusted. "Got *creative* with how they were managing people's money. You wouldn't believe how bad it got."

"This is very harsh," I said, not really thinking.

"Oh?" the local said. "Lass, if they'd burned down a village, leaving all the folk alive without homes or businesses, they'd have done less harm. Let them swing, I say." This world took a very dim view of bankers in general, and those who wrecked people's lives in particular. It wasn't short to say that it was a hated profession.

We couldn't leave without attracting attention, but it still bothered me. I'd seen people die, but this, even if the world thought it was deserved, still hurt to watch. The worst part was that the people cheered as one by one they were dropped, but at least it was a quick and clean death.

Once it was over, we left. I had little desire to stay with the crowd.

CHAPTER 7

ON THE ROAD

After a couple of days of setting up in the capital, it was time to hit the road once more. First, we had to head back to the portal hub to pick up the other end of the portal, then on to Linden.

"So . . . you know anything about the city? Like, what it's like?" Selene asked.

"Dunno. Nobody really talks about it," I responded, which was the truth.

"It's run by the orders, right?"

"Far as I know."

Selene sighed. "Didn't you spend a good part of your childhood with them?"

"A few months."

"So, did they tell you anything about it?"

"Nope. I heard about it during school, and in passing, but not much." I could tell my answers were making Selene slightly suspicious, but I continued. "Honestly, our briefing packet has more than I ever learned."

We'd been given a small overview of our destination, its general location, some basic rules which were just universal, and what we'd be doing.

"That's weird," she finally said, giving up.

"Perhaps, but the priests seem to focus more on the here and now. Far as I can tell, it's one of their central training locations, but it's just administrative, not like, someplace to visit." I shrugged. While I, and a number of bards in general, traveled a lot, that was very statistically rare. If it wasn't to one of their nearest cities, most people only ever traveled for trade or for war.

"Might become a place to visit after we roll through though . . ."

"Perhaps. Maybe that's why Emperor Durin is trying to build relations with them. Then again, it could just be a move for expansion. I bet he wants to grow the empire in this direction in the next few years," I said, theorizing.

"Think he'll go to war with them then?"

"No, Selene, I don't think he will. I think he'll leave them as an independent, or semi-independent city. Everything he's done so far has been by their rules, and nobody, and I mean nobody, wants to go to war with the orders as a whole. Which invading their central training area would definitely start." Priests were typically neutral, but those who had seen them fight wanted nothing to do with that nonsense.

"Is it that bad?" Selene leaned over.

"Never seen one go off on somebody, have you?" I asked.

"Nope." She shook her head.

I sighed. "I've seen it once or twice. It's not pretty, but they've got spells that just, like, kill you. Flesh melting off and stuff. There's probably shields to stop it, and magic resistance of course would help, but when I was young, I saw my friend Kala just end a few guys." While she contemplated that, I briefly wondered how Kala was doing. I hadn't heard from her much. She had a lot of duties to attend to, and her own life now. I told myself I would catch up with her when I got back to Lithere, assuming I could.

We were a few days into the trip. Since it would take several weeks, it was a good chance to work on some of my more practiced spells.

I was in the back of a carriage with Selene, one we'd been given for just the two of us. It slowly bounced down the road, the curtains and storage all secured in place by catches and ties. The gate was stored underneath in a well-hidden compartment.

For this particular trip, we would need to pass through several cities that were not openly hostile, but were probably watching our empire closely. We'd grown strong fast, and had a decidedly military bent, so anyone on our border would surely worry. That was why the gate was in our things. Nobody sane would try to search the personal effects of what appeared to be two young, foreign noblewomen—it would be a national incident. The fact that we didn't have nobles as such wasn't important, it was the implication that was.

On a whim, I decided to go for a walk alongside the carriage. From what I'd seen, the weather outside was lovely and clear, so there was no real reason to stay cooped up. The bright sun shone down on us as we moved, the caravan keeping pace beside me.

We had over a dozen carts in this group, all well maintained and flying the flags of the Empire of Shadows. I'd counted almost a dozen knights as well. They appeared weak at casual inspection, but were all suppressing their power. Even then, a dozen physical magic users, even weak ones, would be a terrifying show of force for any of the city-states along our path. It wasn't enough to count as a military attack, but it would certainly draw eyes.

There are multiple ways to hide something. You could try for straight subterfuge— make the thing invisible and try to avoid getting too close. You could also hide it in plain sight—slip in by making sure you're seen, but keeping your motives unknown. The gate was important, and big, so after much discussion with the higher-ups, it had been decided that it would be hidden among a diplomatic delegation to the city of Linden.

Emperor Durin's good relationship with the priests was well enough known that it would be no surprise that we were sending someone, in this case several someones, of import to talk to the leadership of the orders. Marks and letters detailing our trip and ostensible intent were acquired, and messengers were dispatched to each of the cities we were passing through. The administration of Linden had even gifted us with paperwork detailing that all members had sworn to make no aggression toward those whose lands we were passing through during our trip. Which we had to do before a priest of the Shield.

Our final mode of protection was at the very front of the line. It wasn't a long walk from the center, where my own accommodation was, but enough to give me some fresh air. Here was a carriage, shining bright in white and blue, a stark contrast to the ever present black of the empire's carriages. Its flag was different too, an old symbol I'd first seen long ago, on a medallion around the neck of the man sitting on one of the benches.

"Good afternoon, Rosk. Or should I start calling you Father Rosk now?" I asked as I approached the man.

Rosk had aged since our first meeting. I supposed I had too, though it didn't really feel like it. The once-young priest who stood strong, was now a slightly more grizzled-looking man, with the faintest hints of gray seeping in on the sides of his face. He still had a kind smile, and the bearing of someone dedicated to his fellow man. Age had done him well.

"Just Rosk is still fine, though after I'm finished with this trip, I will have earned the former. Should I be giving you one too, then? Lady Alana, or something like that?" he joked.

"Please no, I'm nothing special," I said.

"Oh, that I highly doubt. Care to join me?" He indicated an open spot on the bench beside him.

"Certainly," I answered as I climbed up. "I wanted some air and the morning is lovely."

"It is indeed," he agreed.

We sat in companionable silence, letting the birds chirp and flutter about.

"Do you expect any problems?" I finally asked, breaking the silence.

"No, not as long as everyone behaves." He gave me a look like I was some kind of miscreant.

"Pfft, like I go about causing trouble." That got a laugh out of him. "We've come a long way, haven't we?" I asked.

"From you singing in a tavern to feed your starving village? I suppose so. Though I do regret some of what was lost on this path."

I nodded at the priest's words. We were never friends, but it was nice to meet old acquaintances from times long past.

"Mind if I ask you something?" I asked.

"Not at all."

"Did you come along because we've met before?"

Rosk laughed. "I do believe a certain bishop assigned me to join this expedition for just that reason. Not that I wouldn't eventually have needed to come this way on my own."

"Meddling jerk," I muttered under my breath.

"I know you two dislike each other, but in this case, I don't believe he meant it as a slight. I merely was available at the right time, and he knew we had a history. He may even be trying to repair the bridges you two so thoroughly burnt." I was still thinking on his words when he spoke again. "Ah, I may have been mistaken."

I looked up in confusion, following his eyes down the road. I didn't see much of note, but apparently I was the only one missing something. The guards perked up and closed ranks.

"Er . . ." I looked about.

"Cloud of dust, Alana. Look there. We have incoming riders—a lot."

There certainly was a haze in the air. "We're not in our own territory, we should be near—" I started.

"A small city-state, Westwood. We're perhaps three hours from the city proper," he rattled off like it was memorized.

"Is it an attack?" I asked, humming up some shields.

"We shall certainly see," he said glancing down at me. Remember your promise to my order, Alana, cast nothing aggressive unless attacked first."

"Don't worry. It's just shields," I responded, a bit of acid in my voice at being spoken down to again.

"Ah, apologies, then. Shields are a rather good move."

I watched the little cloud of dust get closer and closer, eventually coming together as a line of mounted men approached us. There were a lot.

CHAPTER 8

✦

WESTWOOD'S SOLDIERY

The approaching rides were a few minutes away. The knights stayed alert, but none moved to attack, instead falling back into one of many standard defensive formations. Because of the angle of the approach, I could only guess at their size.

One of the knights, an older, gnarled-looking man, rode up beside the carriage, looking over us. I knew he was nominally in charge and that his name was Ernest—Sergeant Ernest to his men. We hadn't said more than a few niceties to each other, as he seemed more business-like than I was. If anything, I got the feeling that he looked down on the less-than-rigid discipline of casters like myself who weren't in the military.

"You haven't retreated to your carriage, Miss," he said as he approached.

"Should I be?" While his form of address had been polite, his surprise that I was not yet hiding ticked me off.

"Most would, but for the moment I doubt they're too much of a threat. If you have some kind of shield, you might want to put that up."

"Already done, Sergeant." We stared at each other for a few moments, neither backing down.

"My estimate is just over a hundred and fifty riders. Now, if West-wood has decided to try and take us, they might have enough casters and knights to do some damage. More than likely though, there aren't many, if any, in this unit. If that's so, my men and I can cut them down like grass before a scythe." He took a quick look at Rosk's face and amended, "If they attack first, of course."

"If things go bad, do you want me to attack?" I asked.

He considered this for a moment. "If there's an opening on one of their magic users and you get a good shot, go for it. But it might be better to save mana for injured men and animals if it goes south. Do you have any decent combat magic?"

"A bit," I answered, more than a bit cross about being questioned.

"I'll leave the decision to you, then." He squinted. "Soldiers, not bandits. They've got uniforms on, local ones."

I was a bit irked at his dismissiveness. I'd fought men and monsters and survived. Did he know that though? Or did he just think I was some little rich girl being sent on an administrative job. It was often hard to tell, since everything was need-to-know and nobody was supposed to speak about it. So there was no way to know if he was actually unaware of who I was or just a patronizing jerk.

As the column of men approaching spread out, it started to matter less. We'd only seen a few travelers on our march, and all who were nearby had booked it. My guess was that they knew that this could be bad and had smartly wanted nothing to do with it.

Unlike our standard black, these men wore a mix of dark red and gold in a checkered pattern. I was glad that they were widening their lines, as it gave me a chance to look them over. With a small hum, I made a light voice appear just over the sergeant's shoulder.

"Two magic users—the leader and the man third to his right," it whispered to him, drawing a chuckle in response.

The two I spotted were both dressed as knights, not that that meant anything. The former was clearly the most important of the men here, with a pressed uniform, more armor, and a fancier helmet. While it was impossible to tell exactly how strong he was—suppressing your aura was standard military practice when first meeting—I got the feeling he wasn't that strong. The other was dressed as any other of these outriders, but about a head taller than the rest.

While the soldiers were clearly stressed, everyone was still holding in place. It took a few moments for the newcomers to look over our banners and process the group approaching their city.

The leader eventually strode forth, looking at us suspiciously. "Greetings, who is in charge of this caravan?" he inquired.

I exchanged looks with the sergeant, only to get a smile and slight nod toward myself. Since this was supposed to be a diplomatic trip, I was the best to take on that particular role.

"That would be me. Is there a reason you brought so many soldiers out to meet us?" I asked.

"Ah, we received a report of a heavily armed caravan flying the colors of another state, so we came to investigate," he said with a slight smile.

"Were you not informed of our passage beforehand? Messengers and approvals were sent, of course," I said, trying to sound as nonchalant as possible.

His smirk was annoying, as was the manner in which they were delaying us. This was clearly about trying to show some kind of power against our empire, which could—and probably would—crush them in the coming years. For now though, I needed him to underestimate me, in case things went south. I could already sense Rosk's irritation. They'd agreed to let us pass with him, so this was just a nuisance; one that could, in some circumstances, lead to needless conflict—something his order was never altogether happy with.

"I can't remember such a thing. Perhaps the paperwork was lost somewhere. If you would be so kind as to come with us back to the city, I'm sure we can find everything we need." He kept up in that same manner, poking and prodding.

"We're headed to the city anyway. It's no issue for us to travel together," I said as I tapped my chin, pretending to think about it.

"Of course, of course, and if you could surrender your weapons . . ."

"No," I cut him off before he could continue. "I'm afraid that isn't possible."

"Unfortunately, we can't just allow an armed force into our lands like this, you understand. While I do not doubt your pure intentions," he offered in a way that made my skin crawl ever so slightly, "I must insist on it. And we will use force, if necessary."

I spent several moments pondering just how funny his face would be when he realized that the small unit of soldiers with me were *all* magic users, and that I was a competent battle-mage. Against a normal group, he probably would have succeeded, perhaps even going so far as to try and keep several of us as hostages. Sadly for him, it was not to be.

"I would advise against that," Rosk interjected.

"And you are?" the soldier asked, clearly unhappy with the interruption.

"Rosk, priest of the Shield," he said loud enough for the nearby soldiers to hear, while revealing the medallion he wore. That cooled everyone quickly. Most people didn't want to cross a caster, and most casters didn't want to cross a priest.

"The orders are neutral though. You're not implying that you would fight with these trespassers?" Even as he said it, I could see the flinch. He hadn't been expecting this particular escort.

"No, not unless my person or carriage were directly threatened. I would, however, be required to report your actions to my order. Attacking diplomats is considered an inappropriate move, is it not? Particularly those who've gone so far as to swear nonaggression." Rosk gave him a concerned look. "That would be horrible, wouldn't it?"

The man was completely thrown off. "Perhaps it would be best if I sent a messenger to confirm then . . ."

"Oh, that would be lovely," I agreed.

One of his men departed. It would be hours before he returned. It would take our carts hours to make that trip, and while he'd surely be quicker as a lone rider, it would still be a long outing.

We gathered for a small lunch, which I invited Ernest to join me for. It disgusted me to do so, but when he seemed to hesitate, I pouted. That delivered the message.

"I don't know what he's up to, but I don't like it," I said after putting a privacy barrier up.

"Agreed. I suppose that's the reason for the dumb girl act?" The sergeant mused.

"Yup. Not sure what his plan is, but I want no part of it. I'd appreciate it if you played along, but feel free to act irritated about it, though."

He scoffed. "All right, lass, but be careful."

"No worries there."

It took the better part of the day for the messenger to return, and then for us to make our way toward Westwood. Their soldiers, even after the confirmation, still formed a column around us, because "they were heading back anyway" and it was "for our own protection" and other platitudes. The leader of their little group did eventually introduce himself as Morian once all the niceties were finally exchanged.

"Again, my apologies for the misunderstanding. Could I perhaps suggest an inn for you and your people? We have quite a few nice ones," he said after our party had finally reached the gate.

Westwood was quaint. It was a middle-sized city, with strong walls and a fortified natural geography that I guessed had really helped it maintain its independence. While it didn't look trashy, I sincerely doubted that they had more than one or two inns of any real quality.

"Oh no, sorry. We'll just send a few of our porters to refresh supplies and then head on. I wouldn't want to bother any of your people, and we are behind schedule." I was lucky I had a smile on, because I came really close to laughing at the face he made.

If the message wasn't clear enough, our porters returned at an almost unbelievable speed. Not stopping for the night, particularly this late, was odd. This was one of the larger cities in the area and would normally be considered safe, as well as a good place to relax before going back to work. But due to my instructions, we didn't even take the caravan into the city proper.

"You're not worried about my men being unhappy skipping the city?" the sergeant asked after we'd left.

"Would they be more unhappy when Morian found some reason to try something?" I retorted.

The old warrior lifted one lip in a crooked smile. "Won't have good beds, nor anyone to warm them out here. Won't be easy to split up either though, eh?"

"Exactly."

Morian

Morian cursed and kicked the wall. Every city of note had factions vying for control, and his was no different. Westwood, for all its glory, was still only one city, but this had been an opportunity. A message passed through from outside to one of their leaders, its source unknown to him. They were to try and detain this passing caravan, easily achieved without the priest's untimely intervention. If that failed, searching them would be the next best thing, but they hadn't even entered the city. He barely managed to delay them for even a few hours.

There were other ways though, and other connections. At the very least, that girl had been some kind of noble. If he managed to capture her and trump up some charges, she could be sold back to her family for a hefty sum. With her attitude, she'd be easy to keep locked up for a while.

"Still mad, boss?" his second asked. The large man didn't look it, but he was sharper than most.

"They got away," Morian responded.

"Aye, and that girl was right cute, eh?"

"She's a noble, my friend. If anything untoward were to happen to her, her family would likely go to war. Keep that in mind."

"Yeah, that wouldn't be good. But we still want to get them, right?" the giant inquired.

"We do. Can I leave it to you and your men?"

"No problem, boss. No problem at all."

CHAPTER 9

✦

ROADS AND MISDIRECTIONS

On the outer edges of Westwood territory

The camp sat upon the edge of an open field—standard protocol. Circled around a cooking fire were a few guards spread out watching the various approaches. It had been easy to follow them here; they hadn't even tried to hide the marks of their passage along the road, or toward this little offshoot.

I whistled one of several calls standard to birds in this area who only sang in the morning, something only locals would realize. While I might be a soldier sworn to a noble family, operations like this weren't too out of place. The only thing we really had to worry about was the priest, and we'd be in and out quick—too quick for him to do much more than kill a few soldiers. That was fine. Everyone here was disposable, and they all knew it but were paid well enough for the risk.

My orders were clear, handed down from my captain, and on to him from another. It didn't matter who or why. All I needed to do was wait and act when the time was right. Get in, kill as many as possible, and grab the noble girl. Those were our orders. I wasn't sure who wanted her, but they wanted her unharmed—lucky for her, but not so much for any other women the men might grab during our little raid.

Looking up at the sky I saw the clouds; even they were perfect. By my guess, we were in for rain, which would handily cover our tracks. Everything was easy, so very easy, like the world itself was egging us on toward victory.

The commander, far from my position, let out a battle cry and we were off. I plunged through the bushes surrounding their camp with a smile on my face. The guards were slow to respond. One looked up and pulled the little bow he had by his side.

As the arrow loosed, something felt wrong, but I couldn't place it. Was it the way the arrow flew? Perhaps he was using an item to change something . . . the sound? Why had the bow not *twanged*? Why wasn't the fire crackling? Why couldn't I hear *anything* other than the mutter of voices?

As my blade reached him, it slid into the guard like he wasn't even there. Literally. Nothing but air met the steel and the thrust, so it threw my balance right off. I could tell from the surprised sounds around me that I wasn't the only one thrown off either.

"Trap!" the commander screamed, a second too late.

A giant spear of white light fell from above, so bright it was painful to look at. The bolt missed. As I turned, my eyes bulged. The men who'd not been so lucky left nothing but smoking ruins.

I had to run from this oncoming death. My breath, so easy a few short moments ago, now came in ragged, panicked gasps as I turned to bolt for the tree line. But before I could reach it, a wall of fire cut off my route to freedom.

Alana

I didn't enjoy killing. Something about the way people screamed when they died, or realized that they were going to, cut deep into my heart. This world was hard , and those men wouldn't have hesitated to pillage, kill, or do any other horrible things to anyone they could have gotten their hands on.

Selene, on the other hand, had a look of hatred on her face as she cast spell after spell. The walls of flame to keep them in had been inspired, and looked more like Dras's handiwork.

"Been practicing fire?" I asked.

"Yeah, got some time recently and some good pointers. Seemed like the right moment to loose it on some deserving bastards." She smiled, looking sinister as the orange light played over her soft features and messy hair.

"No mercy, huh?"

"Think they'd have shown us any had they won?" she replied as she looked up. One of the men had leapt through her wall of fire, and with a casual flick of her wrist she sent a spear forward to immolate him.

I snorted. "You remind me of a priestess I used to know."

Before long, the sergeant joined us from our vantage point nearby. He was wiping the blood from his sword like it was nothing but a small stain. While before he'd been pushing down on his power, I could see some of it now. A bright streak floating in the air behind him like liquid flowing over stone.

"That was embarrassing," he said as he approached us.

"Um?" I had no context for it.

"Their skill, their operation. Heck, their signals were so obvious it was painful. I don't know how the old Ermathi bastards didn't take these fools, but if and when it comes to blows, our men will crush them." We all knew that it was only a *when*, not an *if*, but for the priest's sake he acted as if there was a possibility of peace.

"I don't suppose you captured any?" I asked. Our priest friend would surely be interested in talking to any captives.

"No. Might have, but after you ladies cooked several of them, the rest were too afraid to surrender. They knew their fate even if they did, and men like that don't give up."

"Shame," Selene said, though her cold tone betrayed her.

"Think we'll have these problems in every city?" I asked.

"Well, we've got ten more city-states between here and Linden, suppose we'll find out."

Unknown, Lode's Point

I nodded to my partner. It'd been a long night and we couldn't get to the main target, but this one would have to do. She was not the diplomat, but some kind of assistant or something, and surely worth taking.

What was she doing down in the slums, though? Was this some move by their empire against the city? Our walls and the sheer mountain slopes had always served us well, but if they had some plan, we needed to know.

As we and our counterparts on the other side pulled into the alley though, the girl was gone. Just gone, how? It all started mattering a lot less as something slammed through my back and out my chest.

Spatha

Men rushed in from all sides into the stable. The city guard were out in force against these outsiders, and we'd be taking them in. The little pouch of contraband rolling around my bag would see to that.

"All right, where did they go?" asked the guard captain moments later.

"Sir, how did they go? We've been watching this place all night, nobody's come in or out." I responded.

I spent the next several days trying to find a trace of the caravan, or how they'd slipped from the building and out the gates without anyone seeing. Heads would roll when the traitors who'd aided them were found.

Polipol

Tonight was simple enough; get in, grab the girls, and get out. The extra guards they'd hired to watch their door were just foolish. As if they thought we couldn't put a few mercenaries in our own city on our payroll.

As my men and I crashed through the door to their room, we found no girls, rather several armored and highly angry-looking men with swords. Poor Peter swung down from the roof, right through the window and into the waiting arms of one of their brutes.

Alana, Logista

I stared down from an unassuming room as the would-be assailant slammed his weapon into our man.

"Hey, look at that, those are the sedative sticks used by the capture units back home," I mused aloud to Selene.

The man panicked as the girl he thought he was after turned into an irate soldier.

"I can't believe you told him he had to wear that over his armor for the illusion to take," she responded, looking at the poor man.

"I can't believe we found a dress that big and that frilly," I replied.

"Someone's grandmother is surely missing it." We both winced as the pink abomination over his armor was torn asunder in the violence that followed.

I, not for the first time, regretted that there were no cameras to catch these moments.

Alana, just outside Linden

Rosk looked at me with tired eyes. The horses were showing it too. A few had even been quietly traded out after getting too worn during this trip.

"Nobody who gets near us is going to be fooled by that, you know this right?" He looked me over once again.

I brushed off my clothes again. I was currently dressed as a peasant farmer, and a man at that. It was one of several guises I'd taken up on this overlong trip. Once, I could pass as a boy easily enough, but nowadays my body was too distinctly feminine, and without a lot of artifice there was only so much I could do.

"It only has to work from a distance, and I can toss up illusions to make it work better, like with the carts," I mused while chewing on a piece of grass.

The caravan had gone through a number of changes. Sometimes we avoided all others, sometimes we went forth in all our full regalia. I'd even been working on hiding us, but with the size and movement, illusions were quite difficult to keep up for any amount of time and wouldn't hold up to real scrutiny, particularly in the light of day.

"I'm glad this is nearly over," he said for what had to be the twentieth time.

"Me too. Don't think I've ever been this popular before," I agreed.

"Someone is clearly after us, Alana, you in particular. I can't even say that they'll give up after you're done with your work in the city, and I won't be with you on the way home, should anything go wrong."

"Noted, but don't worry." Our gate, and my way home, wouldn't be in the walls, but it would be near enough to the city that there should be no problems when it came time to leave. I just needed to make it through all the actual talks.

CHAPTER 10

HISTORY LESSON

The walls of Linden were magnificent. Most of the places we passed through, almost all of them in fact, had been unimpressive. This, however, was a very welcome change. I could practically feel the weight and power of ages as we approached defenses that had been built and built over who knew how many years.

There were layers and layers of walls, and even on the approach to the city proper I could see the different styles and types of materials that were used. That struck me as odd, since most places would at least try to normalize their buildings over the years, but here it worked. Each addition seemed designed to keep not invasions of men, but rather monsters from attacking the city.

As we passed through a series of gates, I noticed the buildings looked mostly new. After all, ancient structures did degrade over time—particularly smaller ones—and so building layer on top of layer wasn't too odd. While I had no need to ask, and no plan to look, it wouldn't have surprised me if the undercity of this place rivaled or exceeded that back home.

Thanks to Rosk, we passed through without any problems. The districts got nicer the closer you got to the city center, and it was clear where the actual heavy policing was done to keep crime pushed back to the edges—with the exception of the innermost district where the gates weren't closed.

Our accommodations were in the side wing of an absolutely massive temple. While it had certain sections that displayed the standard architecture I associated with the orders, it featured none of the symbols.

I saw the red curtains of the Lovers, the calm austere outside of the Shield, a garden entrance for the Vine, and strangely, hidden off to one side, a road that led to a tiny temple—one I didn't recognize. It was plain, but not imposing, and the stone path, looking more like a road than anything else, was the only real thing that stood out.

We were greeted at the entrance by a woman in simple but well-made clothing, who smiled brightly.

"Greetings, I hope your trip went well," she said.

"No, in fact, we had a large number of issues on the way. Let's talk inside," Rosk said.

Several of the knights joined us, while several more stayed behind to guard the caravan, taking up defensive positions.

"Someone leaked how important this mission is," I said plainly once we'd been taken inside and sat down.

"I'm not reading into that, Miss . . ." the question obvious on the priestess's voice.

"Alana. And that's not too surprising. We've had issues with security. Many of the cities we've stopped in have either attempted to waylay or attack us, and my worry is that we might not be safe here."

"I'll pass your concerns upward to the city leadership. As for now, I can't tell you too much about the warding or defensive structures of this building, but I can tell you that it is extensive. I can also assign servants who know some of the hidden escape routes in case anything does go wrong."

The sergeant joined us at the table and smiled, taking the lead with a nod. "That would be appreciated, lady . . ."

"Sarah. Sister Sarah, please," she corrected.

"Apologies, Sister Sarah. Could we also request inner rooms without windows? Ideally without hidden entrances to the actual room." He knew security better than I did, so it only made sense to let him take the lead here.

"An odd request, but one that we can meet. Some of them may be small, as those are normally staff quarters. But if that is no issue . . . ?"

It wasn't, and after the sergeant asked for a few more concessions, we were shown to our quarters. It looked like a dorm suite, separate bedrooms all around a central area with easily watchable points of entry. There were even a couple of maids and manservants; something the orders didn't normally avail themselves of, but kept around for visitors like ourselves.

Once everything was in place and a few personal effects had been brought in, I could finally relax. My next meeting wasn't until the following day, and the more important parts had already been taken care of earlier. If we were attacked at this point, there really wasn't anything else we could do. Plus nobody in their right mind would attack the very core of the priestly orders.

The next day was fairly relaxed. My meeting wasn't until well in the afternoon, so I got to see a fair amount of the larger temple complex. There wasn't much else to it, to be honest, since it was mostly used for training and administration. A knight had been assigned to guard me, but he didn't say much.

There were, of course, other temples in the city to deal with things like healing, and any other business that a city of this size might need. But this place wasn't for that. If anything, it was more like the mix between a city hall and a college. Half of it was devoted to teaching priests who couldn't get basic magical training elsewhere, and more advanced students aiming to reach higher like Rosk. The other half was dominated by scribes, actuaries, and offices for the city leadership. There was some overlap, but less than I might otherwise have expected.

I enjoyed a few hours of examining the architecture and the way of life in the temple. It was through that light wandering that I found my way to a massive domed room. It may have served some other purpose in the past, but now functioned only as a crossroads in this facility, and one not often used.

There were many mosaics on the wall depicting some kind of war. But it wasn't anything I recognized. Not only was that odd, but one of the sides seemed to be primarily Elven in nature. The pointed ears were a dead giveaway.

There was a problem, though, and one that had been mounting for a few minutes now.

"Are you okay? You look absolutely pained. If something's wrong I can help, or we could definitely find a priest," I said to the knight.

The guard grimaced. "Don't think that's needed, ma'am. Just . . . just my stomach is killing me. Has been for a good bit now. May—"

"Then let's find you a restroom or something, shall we?" I approached an old man nearby who was sweeping the floor of the huge room.

"Something wrong, dear?" he asked, voice almost creaking as he looked up.

"Is there a restroom nearby?" I asked.

"Certainly, eastern hallway, third door on the left," the elder said.

"Miss, I can't leave you alone . . ." the knight said, only for him to wince. I decidedly did not want this man to release whatever was bothering him here in the middle of the temple, not when I was as safe as I could be.

"Oh, no worries, son, she'll be perfectly safe. I'll even stay with the young lady till you come back, if that helps." He gave the guard a kindly smile and waved him off.

It wouldn't really help, at least not probably. I could see no aura around the man, and even if there was, he wasn't one of ours. Another spasm seemed to make up the knight's mind for him.

"Miss, you stay here where there's lots of people around. If something happens, the sergeant'll have my head."

After a quick nod and eye roll from me he left, looking uncomfortable as he ran for the lavatories.

The old man laughed. "Youngling, there's no danger here." After we shared a quick snicker, he looked up. "I saw you looking through the old murals."

"I was. I've never seen their like before. What are they about?"

"Ah," he said, moving over to the wall. As he did, I couldn't help but notice that despite his apparent age, this man looked strong and very healthy. "These are about the founding of the orders."

"I don't think I know that story . . ." I mused.

"Well, we don't tell it much. There's a certain caution that it could inspire hatred, which we'd rather like to avoid, and it is really ancient history." At my raised eyebrows and interest, he continued, leading me back to the beginning of the show to start.

"Roughly five thousand years ago, man lived in the dirt and stones. In that time we were truly primitive, living in caves and huts without metal or great buildings like we have now," he began as we looked at an image of people looking something like cavemen.

"From the far west a different people came, bringing knowledge, teachings, and buildings, but also ruling."

"Elves?" I wondered as we walked along, seeing ships and their passengers landing upon shores that were surely supposed to be from this continent's.

"Yes, elves. They came, and while they brought knowledge and more magic than most men had at that point, they also ruled, making it clear that they were the only ones to be followed."

But they didn't now. I knew there had been a war, and things had happened that bothered ancient Justin, but I didn't know the details.

"Things went, well, not too terribly for a time. Certainly, the elves governed us humans, but not too harshly. Then something happened. Few know, or knew, I am told, the full details, but there was some tragedy, and the leader of their people went mad."

We kept moving and I saw him there. Whoever had first made this had to have met the old elf, or gotten a very, very good description, because here, in one of the images I had missed, stood Justin. He looked like an exact copy, and even his aura was depicted properly. There were differences though. He stood encased in armor, a war hammer in his hand and a snarl of pure hatred on his face; a look I couldn't really associate with the man I'd met.

"He destroyed a city wholesale, thousands dead in only a day as fire and death rained upon the people. It didn't end there, though. The leaders who'd been hard but not cruel changed their ways. They began to oppress; any dissent crushed beneath the heels of Elven soldiers."

The next image showed just this. Cities burning, people dead and dying in the street, or otherwise weeping.

"It started with a group of four, four priests who couldn't abide the oppression any longer. Together, they came and met with their followers, forming a true resistance."

I had to stop him here. There was a depiction of four people, that was true. The first, a large man with a shield in his hand, who stood strong like a hero, who was oddly familiar. Beside him was a smaller, lithe man surrounded by plants crawling up his arms. The third was odd.

"An Elven priestess?" I asked. The beautiful woman who was shown there was clearly no human.

"Indeed, one of those who joined to fight back was an elf. She'd seen the depredations and dedicated herself to the protection of the women and babes who had been predated upon. That is the founder of the Order of Lovers."

He must have seen my shock and allowed time for it to sink in. The last figure was small, and also a man, his face half covered by the shadow from his hood.

"Who is that?" I asked, nodding.

"That is the founder of the Wanderers."

"I've never even heard of them," I said.

"Not surprising," the old man replied. "They're few and far between. They mostly dedicate themselves to exploration and the furthest edges of the civilized world. We train a handful every few years, but even this place seldom sees that order. If we do, it's only for short period of training. Then they go off on their business, only infrequently reporting back on their findings."

Further down was an image of a titanic battle.

"The priests of the orders and all of their followers finally began to drive his armies away, freeing the lands. Not much is known about what happened after the final battle. The elves claimed that their master survived, leading their forces home before disappearing. Regardless, when the dust settled, the elves fled in total, leaving the lands."

"And I'm guessing that this place was built not long after?" I postulated.

"Correct. In fact, this is the spot of that last struggle. At least that's what the records say." He gave a smile. Ancient history was sometimes hard to pin down, but I was inclined to believe it.

I could see the knight returning, looking relieved.

"Thank you, sir, for your time," I said. "Ah, may I know your name?"

"Oh, most people just call me elder, my dear, but feel free to call me Aaron. At least in private." He conspicuously tapped the side of his nose and winked.

"Then thank you, Mister Aaron. Sadly, I think I must go."

"You're quite welcome, Alana. Have a wonderful afternoon," he bade me as I went to go join my guard. There were other places to go today.

Elder Aaron

A few moments after they left, the old priest sighed, finally able to relax.

"Everything well, Elder?" asked an aide who'd been waiting down one of the paths.

"Fine, fine, just that holding in my aura is tiring on these old bones of mine." I gave one of my favorite excuses, even though I hadn't aged in a very, very long time.

I resumed sweeping, watching the golden bubbles of my aura bounce off the ground. Some of my students and acolytes would frown seeing me do menial labor like this, but it helped me keep pride away. I liked reminding myself of where I came from, and not acting like one of those foolish kings.

"Did you get what you desired?" the aide asked, following behind me, careful not to mess up my cleaning.

"Not all of it, but I got to take her measure. It is enough."

"Can I get you anything else, then?"

"You certainly can, lad," I said. "A dustpan would be quite useful."

CHAPTER 11

✦

LOSING A FRIEND

I still had a fair amount of time before the meeting, but I made my way to the location. I needed to make a good impression, and tardiness would certainly do me no favors. Selene joined me, and we found ourselves in a waiting room of simple, yet extremely well-made, furniture.

The orders frowned upon displays of excess, but that didn't mean they were poor. There was no gold filigree or silver, no velvet or lace to be found, but tables and chairs were finely crafted and comfortable—at least moderately so. Art was sparse, but each piece was quite detailed. Even the breakfast I'd been given this morning was cooked with high-quality ingredients.

There was no hiding that I was fond of food. I paid a lot of attention to what I was eating, regardless of where I was. Nearly starving as a child had killed any pickiness that I might have felt, but it was still important to me to look at my food, appreciate it, see what I could learn about what it was and how it was prepared. The dishes here were mostly fruit and porridge, but it was all made with a practiced hand that was well-versed in how to precisely mix for proper flavor.

My rumination on food was broken when the door opened.

"The elders will see you now," a young man said, leading us into the meeting room.

Seated around the table were a handful of older people, each in their own robes. A man with grey hair and broad shoulders gave us a harsh look, narrowing his eyes above the symbol of the Shield. Beside him sat an elderly woman who exuded a scent of earth and leaf litter for the Vine. A woman who was visibly younger than her fellow elders was clearly here to represent the Lovers, her hair still a dark chestnut brown. The last wiry man looked like he wanted to be anywhere but here, his leg bouncing like he'd been forced to sit still in a place he found intensely boring.

Below the priests were a few administrators—I was guessing—non-casters and casters whose dress singled them out as decidedly not priests. Those paled next to what I saw at the head, though. Aaron, the old man who I'd met earlier, sat in priestly robes at the seat of honor. I nearly spat out his name but then remembered how he'd said to call him that in private, and held my tongue.

His aura was potent, the golden bubbles flowing off him nearly pushing down those of the other nearby priests. It wasn't quite what I'd seen from a certain elf, but close.

"Am I the only non-archmage?" I whispered to myself, but a few people seemed to catch it.

It was a bit frustrating how all the other people brought to this world seemed to move to the peak of power. I was at least assuming he was a transmigrator, the bubbles seeming to be a dead giveaway to who we were. Then again, if I'd lived for what I was assuming were hundreds of years, I might well have the same kind of incredible power.

Justin had mentioned another, a priest who could probably keep himself young. He hadn't quite managed young, but he was almost certainly the man the wizard had mentioned. As I looked at his eyes, it clicked. The man in the mural who'd seemed so familiar could only be the one sitting here before me now.

"Please join us, ladies, we've much to discuss," he offered.

Selene gave me a sidelong glance, seeming to have heard something of my whisper, but joined me in one of the open seats.

"Certainly, where would you like to begin?" I inquired.

The priest representing the Shield was the first to go. "Most of the important bits have been covered, but let us clarify. We've agreed to this gate only because we will be covering the opening on our end to properly forbid any military use."

"Of course," I answered. "Though the instructions for its use are iron-clad. Emperor Durin has designated it only for trade and limited travel with agreed-upon individuals. Eventually it might be opened to public usage, but that would be in the future once we've got a proper network set up."

Nobody really believed that there wouldn't be some work to make this function for military purposes, even if they were pretty limited, but that was the official line. Personally, I thought that in time we'd be sending extra gates, even small ones, through it to aid in the conquest of some of the local cities. Troops would be impossible though, and there didn't seem to be any plan to attack Linden.

Not because Emperor Durin didn't want to, but because it was insane to do so. Priests didn't normally get involved in wars, but this was their home base, and nobody believed that there wouldn't be some action if someone tried to take it from them. There were a few historical examples of kingdoms and empires that had tried, and it didn't surprise anyone that they'd all ended shortly thereafter.

"I have some questions about the setup and these sequences of wards you've provided," said one of the city leaders, a wizard if I had to guess. "How do we know that you won't change them?"

Selene took this one, as she would be handling some of our security here. "You're welcome to provide them, if you like, or we can leave them to be obscured physically by your people. None of them are state secrets."

That was a concession, but these weren't the same wards we were using around the military gate. They weren't even anything special, just a few shields and the like, all blocking things from exiting the inside too quickly. We were using quite a different set on our side, though.

"Will there be any objections if we set up our own afterward?" the man continued.

"Not so long as they fall within the agreed-upon forms. The facility is under your control, of course, but so is ours. Either side will be able to end the linkage," Selene answered with a shrug.

"How many others are currently in the network?" one of the others asked. Her glasses and the ink stains on her fingers pointed to some kind of administrative work.

"None, currently," I said. "Though that will be changing. A series within our lands first, then we'll be looking outward again."

"I don't believe for a second that you don't have other gates, young lady. I was asking about those," she said with a frown.

"If there are others, they are not connected to this network," I replied with the line I'd been given should they push for it.

The answer got me another frown. We had others, and they knew it, but I knew that there'd be questions about those.

The administration had a number of questions about the place they would be putting the gate, but honestly all of that was their decision, not ours. We wanted this up; letting them own the location it stood on wasn't the concern. There were only a few requirements: a couple observers from our side, and the room-size specifications. All of that had been accepted in earlier proposals.

The elder priest from the Wanderers struck in once the city admins had finished their questions. "How far can these go?"

"That's currently unknown," I said. "We've not yet hit a location that they can't reach."

"Instant movement to anywhere in the world?" I could see his eyes twinkle as he thought about the possibilities. His order did reach for the edges of the map, so this could really speed them up in some ways.

"Not quite instant. There's a small delay on very long trips," I clarified.

"Hmm? I wonder why," asked the elder for the Lovers.

"Current working theory is to protect causality, but that's not really important. The delay to circle the world would be limited." That was intel, but wouldn't help with the gates, so I had no problem giving it to them.

"Causality?" She seemed confused by my answer.

"The progression of events from one to another. If you were to be able to change that, who knows what destruction might follow," Aaron finally spoke, having been quiet up till this point.

"Um . . . thank you, Elder," I could see that she was still a bit thrown off.

It occurred to me that he'd told me that most called him elder, but I'd been thinking *elderly*. The truth was that he was "Elder," as in the oldest, and probably strongest priest they had bouncing around.

"It would breach into something like time travel, ma'am. Imagine if you were to go back in time and kill your grandfather before your father was born. Then you might never come to be, so you couldn't go back and kill him, so he wouldn't die, so you could, so he would, and so on." The grandfather paradox was an old one and explained the issues with time travel quite simply.

"That sounds . . . like something bad would happen," she said, still trying to come to grips with the concept.

"There have been recorded attempts at time travel and manipulation over the years, all with destructive outcomes. Why would traveling too fast compromise that, though?" their old wizard asked.

"I'm afraid that is a secret. Our government has no desire to see anyone foolishly attempting such things again," I answered. Selene didn't know much about that, but I'd spoken with some of our team about how things didn't travel faster than light before. Not that I had the knowledge to properly explain more than a standard sci-fi show, though.

There was a bit of grumbling, but it was soon interrupted.

"I've only one concern, and questions that I expect you to answer. Where did you get these from?" As the Elder spoke, everyone else fell silent.

I looked to Selene. This wasn't something we'd expected to have to share. There were a few ways to answer, but a lot of that consisted of things we really couldn't share. Selene wove a veil of silence around us and leaned in to whisper.

"Not sure how much we can say. Will they let us out without some answer though?" she asked.

"Honestly, I don't know how they'll respond if they don't like what we say, or if they've some way to know if we're lying."

There was a bit of a back-and-forth for a few moments before we decided on what to say. It was a risk, and did reveal some things, but not everything. The real concern was what would happen if we didn't answer at all. Selene unwove the veil of silence.

"Emperor Durin provided the original, an artifact which we then researched to create the current model," I said. A truth, but not much in the way of from where, or whom.

The ancient man narrowed his eyes and thought for a few moments. "I see. To your knowledge, do any others have access to your gate system, particularly other nations?"

He was asking about the elves. No matter how much time had passed, I got the feeling there was still bad blood there; a lot between this old man and the other. More must have happened than the simple explanation I'd been given about that mural.

"No," I answered, a full truth this time. The gate to the Elven lands had been turned off by Justin and was currently off by our own designs.

"Very well," he said after a time, processing my answer and staring me down. "We will need a bit of time to discuss amongst ourselves."

We were shown to the waiting room and had to twiddle our thumbs for nearly an hour. During that time, Selene shot me a few looks but said nothing. It wasn't clear what was up, but she certainly wanted something from me.

Eventually, they gave the final rubber stamp. Everything had been approved already; the details hashed and rehashed out long before we'd ever set out. This was supposed to just be a final talk before work began, a last chance for any questions, but for a bit there it looked like we might have to make the trip home without finishing—something I was really not looking forward to doing.

The day had grown long before it was all done, and when we got back I nearly fell onto my borrowed bed. While lying there, a knock sounded from my door. I opened it to find Selene looking quite bothered.

"May I come in?" she asked, looking around.

"Sure, something up?"

"One moment please." She began casting layers and layers of her own privacy wards. I recognized most of them, having known her for a while now, but some were a mystery to me.

"Okay . . . what's going on?" I said when she looked finished.

She glared. "Alana, what did you mean when you asked if you were the only one who wasn't an archmage?"

That had not been meant for her, or anyone really, to hear.

"Well, we've been meeting a lot of them recently, haven't we?" I tried.

"Alana, I'm not an idiot, nor am I blind."

"Er . . ." I was trying to think of something. I expected that one day my family, or maybe Mystien would start asking uncomfortable questions, but Selene? She'd been there, just . . . in the background, around, a bit of a friend.

"How long have we known each other? That Elder guy, he has the same kind of aura as that terrifying elf, the same aura as you. Now, I'd really like to know, because it looked to me like there was some other communication between you two. He knows something, something you do, and something you're not telling me."

That was not good. If she was seeing this, then someone else might too.

"It's about the aura, Selene. It's like everyone I meet with who is scary and weird," I lied.

"You're weird and scary in your own right, when you need to be. That isn't all though, and this isn't over. There's something up, something about these portals, and I think you know what." We just stared at each other for a few minutes, neither wanting to talk.

"There's some kind of magic going on, something that I don't understand." While that was the truth—I had no idea how we'd all gotten here—it certainly wasn't all of it.

"I see, so that's how it is." With that, she turned on her heel and left, slamming the door behind her.

I waited, waited to see if knights would come to take me, waited to see if there'd be some alert among our people. None came, though. For all that she was clearly pissed, nothing was coming for now. I sighed. I'd need to come up with something, or things would be very, very bad when I got home—if I went home.

CHAPTER 12

✦

ADMISSIONS AND ASSAULTS

Over the next few days, Selene was more distant than usual. She said nothing about our conversation, but looked up harshly at me every now and then. I was glad for that much, as there was more than enough to do.

The place where Linden had elected to set up the portal was a small fortress about half an hour outside of their walls. I knew that many a merchant would someday complain that there wasn't a good place to just get into the city, but the safety concerns were valid. I also imagined that if the city elders hadn't already allocated all the land in the general area to someone, those same merchants would shortly scoop it up by the acre for storehouses, loading docks, and all manner of stables.

That would be their problem though, not mine. For now, all I needed to do was see to the proper installation of things and head home, preferably through the gate that would then be up. The caravan would need to go back the old-fashioned way, with a few different guards and passengers. I'd need to consult with the higher-ups back in the capital, but we could probably arrange for some nasty surprises for those trying to stop them on the way back.

I was still debating if I would be going back, or for how long. There were some very good reasons to never return to Lithere, or perhaps even back to the capital city. If Selene decided that she wanted to bring up her concerns to our bosses, it could end me. Emperor Durin was already displeased, I knew, at my secret keeping, and I didn't know how he'd respond to me keeping anything else from him, not that I was keeping things he had business in.

Would he see it that way though? This really didn't concern him, or his empire, but he'd want to know, and we both knew that. Keeping it to myself would probably be seen in a very dim light. I didn't know how he'd respond, but my guess was not well.

It all depended on Selene; I would need to talk to her. I wasn't sure how the story about being from another world would be seen, but I didn't plan to share that much. I could at least tell her that the three of us, and I suspected others, had an unusual insight into the workings of magic. I could tell her that I didn't know how that happened, which was true. Would she accept that though, or run to tell others that I had odd insights?

As for my current job, it was almost casual. We'd put up a few of these now, and well understood the process. The city itself was more in the way than anything else. Their mages were always buzzing around, doing wards of their own, and examining our actions with an inquisitive eye.

"Could we get more of these?" one said on the third day of work. "They'd be quite useful."

"That would be a question for our government. Sadly, I have no control over where they're going, and in what order," I responded.

"What do you think the chances are, though?"

"Honestly? Low for right now. I think Emperor Durin wants to set up our network first. After we've done that though, still low. These are just a hair's breadth from being military-only technology." I gave him a shrug and the man sighed.

"Figures. Since that's off the table, could you go over these wards with me? I'm concerned about how they'll interact with some of ours." He pulled out a paper detailing one of ours, one I'd made myself.

We spent the next hour going over the details, many of which he couldn't, or wouldn't, share with me, to make sure to check for interaction. As it stood, there was one—one which would slowly damage both of them. It was poor design that I attributed to one of their passed-down protections, something many places kept secret.

Which was stupid. How was I supposed to help with the problem if I couldn't see half of what was going into it? By the end of it, I knew most of what was going into that particular ward anyway, because he had to explain it just for me to check over things. At several points, I nearly told him to sod off and figure it out himself, since he had our wards and should have been able to see the issues, but I held my tongue.

We finished everything late, but that was fine. With everything done, there was only the standard testing to run through in the morning, and then I could go home. I wasn't even going back to my room at the city temple tomorrow afternoon. I was bringing all of my luggage and heading back home.

Emil

I was too old to still be a spymaster, far too old. Sadly, there was nobody else I could properly trust. I needed an apprentice, someone whom I could teach all my methods and leave tasks like this to. Magic user or not, though? If I choose someone without, he'd be honored by the choice and likely take me more seriously. But the power that magic could bring . . .

I had plenty of time to ruminate on this during the trip here, and hopefully would have more on the way back. For now, I had work to do.

Getting messages out to all of those who might be allies in this region had been a pain. The fact that all of them had failed to capture my targets, or even delay them a bit, was irksome, to say the least. Not every leader had a proper spy network, and even if they did, I didn't have connections to all of them.

It mattered little now, as I was in place to see my target as she and her entourage passed through the city gates. I'd managed to learn that they were here to set up some kind of transport system, but I didn't have all the details. Not yet.

I nearly gasped as I saw the girl passing through the gate. My aide had the good sense to wait until they'd well and passed before he spoke.

"You knew her?" The man spoke in a neutral voice; whispering could attract unwanted attention.

"I'll tell you when we get back," I answered.

Alana

"We have our primary target," I began.

"Selene," I continued after putting up a sound barrier, "let's talk." We were sitting atop our carriage, enjoying the afternoon air.

"Oh? You're going to actually answer me now? Not just lie to my face?"

This would clearly be an uphill battle. "Ask what you want to," I replied.

"What is it about you three that is important?" she asked, scowling.

"Honestly? I don't know," I answered, "I do know that all of us have insights, we think differently, and understand each other, and magic, in unusual ways. I suspect Ristolian was the same as well."

"The mage who made the gates? Why?"

"When I was in school, our first dean, Dean Lorrae, told me a story. He told me how he laughed when he received the message upon completing his core. Declaring it all a joke."

She gave me an odd look. "You're not making any sense, Alana."

"It is a joke, though. That message is 'hello world, look at me, I'm working,' to everyone."

She tried to process that for several seconds. She stared, then blinked, then shook her head as if she had a question, then tried again.

"You can understand it? The code. The code that everyone sees but nobody gets, the one in the core!?"

I nodded.

"But . . . but, you know what that whole unknown section says then, don't you? You have to tell!"

"You already know, Selene. Ristolian wrote it down. Those books they gave us, the ones the emperor found—they're guidebooks on how to use the core."

"But that was put there by the core's maker, the king that . . ." She froze.

"Yeah," I confirmed.

I could see her processing. "That . . . that elf we met in that ruin . . . he wasn't just there to clean, was he?"

"No, I don't think so."

"The priest? The old one?" she asked.

"I don't know too much about him, but I get the sense that he really sincerely hates that particular elf. I also think that if those two power-houses tried to raise armies, they would, and the result would be . . ."

"Apocalyptic," she finished.

I gave her a few moments to process. She'd gotten enough to know that I had more understanding of magic than she did, and could read the core, for some reason. There was no point in telling her about another world now. It would only cause issues.

"Now you know, and you know why I don't want anyone else to find out," I finally said.

"I . . . I won't tell a soul. Our lands are right between them. If they decide to fight, we'll be the battlefield, and nobody is ready for war with all of the elves. That's terrifying. Or maybe we should . . . if the emperor knew, he could prepare."

"We're already on the brink of war, Selene. Nothing will change that. They've also been holding their peace for a very long time, and seem to want to continue. Poking and prodding either of them might set it off."

She nodded at my declaration, still looking more scared than I was about that particular possibility. After a few moments she gasped and yelled. I saw her reach down and pull something familiar—and terrifying—from her hand.

"Selene?!" I shouted.

She was holding one of the little dart-like syringes used by our own capture squads. I ducked and shouted, hoping to alert our guards, as two more darts struck the seat behind me.

I felt stupid as I quickly dropped the sound shield, readying to yell again. It wasn't needed though, as the knights quickly recognized the attack.

It was a good opener. Taking down casters was a strong way to start any attack, as it deprived the enemy of ranged support and healing. My blood chilled as I also realized the method of attack indicated their intent to capture, not kill.

I sang my shields into place as the carriage lurched forward with a *woosh*. The *crunch* that followed was our wheel breaking in half. I couldn't see, didn't know what was going on, but I needed to be ready, because from the sound I guessed they had at least one wizard with them.

Selene was struggling, but it was clear that she was losing strength fast. The sedatives in the darts must have been astoundingly potent. In less than a minute. she was struggling to form even the most basic of spells.

I considered using my gate spell, but there was no reason to think anywhere within sight would be safe. Instead, I quickly tossed invisibility over myself and started the process of conjuring up a storm. Lightning might not be the fastest attack at my disposal, but it was the strongest.

As I slipped from my spot, I saw the battle. Our knights were strong, but the enemy had numbers. We were outnumbered at least two to one; the men still standing after the opener fighting were more than one opponent each, and those enemies were magic users too—that much was clear from the speed and strength of the melee.

In the back I could see a few archers and the aforementioned casters picking off targets quickly and with devastating results. That group would have been my first target for some electrical vengeance, but something caught my eye.

Next to one of the casters, a man was pointing directly at me. He had an aura near his eyes like Charles, but significantly weaker.

I tried to dodge before whatever they were planning hit me. As I did, I drew in breath for a scream, letting the storm fall. I needed to hit and fast. If they could see me, they could drop me.

I bounced against some kind of kinetic wall before my dodge was finished, and while that only made me panic more, it did lend itself well to the scream I let loose at the casters. I didn't hold back a bit, and they all flinched. But the wall didn't budge.

This was bad. They'd planned this. They'd planned for me. Someone among them knew my abilities. They were trying to keep me contained.

Spells pummeled my shield in quick succession like hail. None were strong enough to kill, but they were all draining my power. I struggled to keep it in place, pulling in magic for another scream. There was no time for anything else.

One of the warriors broke from the melee and blurred in my direction. His charge hit my shield like a freight train and shattered it. My scream attack landed head-on as he came, but it was cut short when his metal-clad fist planted itself in my stomach.

My feet left the ground, taking me up as I felt a sickening crunch around my ribs. Clinging to consciousness, I seemed to hover in the air. I wanted to scream in agony, but there was no time. Before I even landed, the man tossed me like a rag doll toward his compatriots.

At that speed, it surely would have killed me had I landed, but someone caught me in a cloud of kinetic magic. Before I could struggle, they were upon me, again firing those accursed needles. Three landed in my arms and torso, one more in the thigh—each burned as it landed. Then my body went numb. At least I couldn't feel the broken ribs.

As my mind slipped away, I saw Selene, flying toward us in a mess of hair and fabric. The man who tossed me must have done the same to her. As she landed, I saw her panic and fear as she, too, struggled to stay conscious. A fight we both lost.

CHAPTER 13

✦

CAPTURED

I opened my eyes, looking wearily around the dark room. I couldn't tell where I was, but it was painfully cold. It felt like I had been sedated for weeks. Time had been both infinite and a blur—strange and confusing. Apparently they'd stopped now, and I was beginning to come back to my senses.

There had been occasional points when the sedation stopped. Brief moments when I began to crawl slowly from the blanket of sleep they were forcing on me. I would try to sing the poison in my veins away, only for someone to strike me, or gag me—anything to stop me from casting. During those times I'd been forcibly fed and given water, and at one point even cleaned by some other woman.

Keeping someone drugged forever was impossible though, at least with our level of medicine. There had to be a balance between keeping me helpless and keeping me alive. As each dose of poison had been forced in, my body slowly began acclimating to it. In time I would have gained enough resistance that the sheer amount required to keep me disabled would have killed me.

The fever dream had lasted long enough to transport me readied here. I supposed that was all they really needed in their minds, to keep me down until they could . . . I shuddered to think about what they wanted. Even worse, what they might have done while I was asleep.

I checked my surroundings. Nobody else was in the room, and no one was at the door. I hiked my dress up. My mark was still there upon my leg. Still glowing, though noticeably it was about a month down from its maximum charge. I'd never experienced this kind of fear before, and suddenly felt very much like any girl who woke up after a wild party somewhere she didn't know. Except this hadn't been some fun night out. I lay back and wept quietly, noting, but not caring about, the shackle around my right wrist.

I pushed as much mana as I could into the tattoo I'd gotten so many years ago. A safety I'd hoped would never become as important as it felt in this moment. Eventually it refused to accept any more, pushing back. Probably a safety measure for situations like this one. In time, I fell asleep again, letting the darkness wash over me again.

It was light when I woke up. There were no friends here to help me, no family. What did the people who took me want? Who even were they? Where had they taken me? I needed answers, and I needed them fast.

Now that I could see, it was clear I was in some kind of prison. I was lying on a straw mattress in one corner next to a basin for water and a chamber pot—lovely. I could see a small window from where I struggled to rise.

I wanted to vomit as I labored to pull myself up. The last of the drugs must have been wearing off. I was weak, painfully so, like a baby deer struggling to take its first steps. Eventually I managed to sit up, using the freezing stone wall as a prop.

I was shackled to the ceiling, a long chain running down from an inset loop to the cuff that was tight around my wrist. I tested that to find it was tight, extremely tight, with no easy way to get it off. It didn't seem enchanted, but the walls to this room definitely were. There was just a feeling about it and the way my aura seemed to bounce off of them oddly, never quite touching.

The door looked sturdy—wood with iron bands holding it, and there was a small viewing window, now open. I couldn't see anyone out there, but that didn't mean there weren't guards. Casters were notoriously difficult to contain, particularly for any amount of time. That was the main reason that we were seldom captured, unless we surrendered.

I wanted to see the window first; get a look outside. The guards, whoever they were, would probably make themselves known in time.

I almost fell to the floor as I stood, the whole world lurching. The chain also made a horrid racket as it slid across the floor. That sound made a face appear instantly in the little window, feminine, but hard.

It took only a few seconds for the door to be opened and a pair of guards—all women, I happily noted—to make their way inside. Another remained in the hall, keeping an eye out. I didn't know who these women were, but they were not playing any games.

All three had auras. Nothing impressive, but even a weak magic user was still a magic user. Of them, the leader, an older blonde with a few wrinkles and scars, was the strongest—a cold, steel-colored mist.

"Sit," she instructed.

"What have you done to me?" I asked as I fell back to the bed.

"I believe that is obvious, prisoner." She took another look at my face, the tear streaks from earlier likely still there. "Nothing horrid, as of yet. There are rules, you will listen."

I nodded and she continued. "I've been informed by reliable sources that you are a bard who specializes in song and dance magic. If you attempt to sing, we will take that as a threat. If this chain begins to move too much—" She shook the metal implement, and it loudly clattered. "We will take that as a threat. Understood?"

"Yes. Who are you?" I wanted as much information as I could get.

"You do not need to know that. What you do need to know is that if I or my subordinates catch you trying to cast or escape, we will not be pleased, little girl. You may think that your situation now is bad, but believe me, it can get so, so much worse." Her eyes darkened as she spoke.

"I understand . . . will you at least tell me where I am? Whoever you are, I'm sure that they'll pay the ransom." I didn't know if they'd contacted my family, but most people would. They wanted the money a caster would get when sent back to their family, and I had no doubt that they would really want me back home.

She scoffed. "We are not stupid enough to alert the traitor to your location, fool. Since it will soon become obvious anyway, there is no reason to hide this from you. You are currently in the custody of His Majesty King Lief, the true king of Bergond."

I paled as she turned and shut the door loudly behind her. So far as I knew, nobody knew exactly where the fallen prince had run off to, only that he'd taken a lot of his people with him. I also knew that the chances of them trying to sell me back to my own family were hovering stubbornly right at zero. I was on my own, and I really needed to get out of here.

Several Weeks Earlier

Durin felt his heart thrumming as he read over the report. Just this morning, one of his men, Sergeant Ernest, had stumbled through the brand-new gate to Linden, ignoring the safety checks, and had nearly set off dozens of countermeasures against attack. While the man would need to be chided for his misstep in procedure, he at least had good reason.

Their caravan had been attacked on the way to the gate. Three of his knights, good men, were dead. As for the two casters they were guarding . . . The two girls had been captured in a fast attack. From the looks of it, their opponents had known the capabilities of at least one of them to a T. It honestly looked like something he'd have done, but these were enemies.

They'd managed to kill five of the attacking men but failed to capture any of them. Debriefings would need to happen, and fast. The damage we'd incur from the loss of those researchers could not possibly be understated.

Durin sighed and felt heavy. He also needed to talk to his old friend Verren. The man would not take this well. Hopefully they'd have a target at which he could vent his fury by the time that meeting happened.

CHAPTER 14

✦

OUT OF THE CELL

Being locked up was an all-too-common occurrence in my life. It never got any more fun either, but this was a new low. I was cold, alone, and feeling rather more abused than I would have liked. It also looked like there was little chance of rescue for me unless I was the one doing my rescuing.

Hours ticked by with no interaction. I eventually stood and went to the window, the drugs finally properly wearing off.

At least I had a good view. Sure it was through bars, but it was a good one. The small city outside was covered in snow, almost idyllic in its form. There were lights, and a few people moving here and there within the walls. I was currently at a higher altitude, almost certainly within some kind of castle or fortress that looked down upon the settlement.

I was coming up with a plan, but there were still parts here and there that I needed to work on. I really needed a safe place to teleport to, but finding that was the hardest bit. I didn't know what was where anywhere in this town, and I was leery of doing anything that might make the situation worse. I'd get one escape attempt, and if I screwed it up, I'd likely just be killed.

It was surprising that they were keeping me alive right now anyway, as even if I wasn't me, it would be a damn hard thing to keep going for too long. Most mages would run or fight if they thought they'd be killed, only ever surrendering if it was safe, and I had a strong feeling that they'd get around to putting my head on a pike sooner or later if I stayed.

I spent several days looking over the town, trying to identify the entrances and exits, the buildings of import and what they were. It was hard at this distance, but I was fairly sure that I'd found some kind of storehouse with a broken shutter, and even the direction the traffic was going. There were no gates in the wall from my viewpoint, but that was of little import.

Standing here and watching had become my habit, and there was little to interrupt me. Sometimes the guards would come to check that I was here, or deliver rather poor food, but more often than not I was left to my own devices.

Which made it strange when I heard a jingling and the noise of a key being put into a lock. At first I didn't turn around, figuring it was the guards either bringing me something or about to do something unpleasant, neither of which I was terribly interested in.

"Hello, Alana, it's been some time, hasn't it?" a slightly familiar male voice said.

I turned to see the face of a man I hadn't seen in years, not since the fall of Lithere.

"Professor Rooke?" I asked, confused.

He gave me a smile. "Indeed. I'm glad to see you remember your old teacher."

"Come to interrogate me?"

"In a sense, yes. I am hoping that I can convince you that won't be necessary." At my raised eyebrow, he continued. "Your situation is . . . severe, as I'm sure you well know, but His Majesty isn't an unkind man, nor one without reason. He remembers you from that little adventure you had as children, and would really rather not see you harmed. May I sit?"

He indicated a small stool, something the guards had delivered with the food this morning. At my nod, he took a seat. I settled down opposite him, looking at a man who'd aged considerably since I'd been in school. His robes were now thick, and not quite as . . . well-made? Not as fancy at any rate.

"I didn't know that you two knew each other," I stated.

"Until the capital fell, I'd only met him a few times at formal functions, but even then I knew he was a decent young man, and he hasn't disappointed me at all."

"So what? You just expect me to give you . . . what do you want anyway?" I asked.

"We know that you were involved in some project in Linden, though not the exact nature. We want the information on that, as well as the sky-metal. If you cooperate, I've been told that you'll find your . . . accommodations will improve drastically, and you'll be given a second royal pardon. Living as you did didn't indicate any disloyalty, but rather a need for you to survive in the new era." I sat still as he made his pitch, unsure if I should believe it or not.

"You know that my father and brother are both heavily involved in the empire's army, do you not?" I asked.

"I do, and it is unfortunate, and there may be something that can be done for them if they surrender. I think you should start thinking of yourself though, Alana." The threat was clear.

"If I accept?"

"You'd be held here for the duration of our war, but as I said, in a much more pleasant place. When it's all said and done, you'd be allowed to return to the country proper, free and clear."

"And should I refuse?" I asked, interested in what they had planned.

"That is more complicated. It would depend on how long you refused."

That sent a chill down my spine and I struggled to think. I needed to get out of here, now.

"You won't help me, will you?" I asked.

"If you don't cooperate, I'm afraid I cannot, and will not." We sat in silence for several minutes after that, me thinking and him watching my reactions, before he finally continued. "Take a few hours to think on things, Alana. If you decide to help me, and yourself, let the guards know."

He left me, and while I'd like to say that I wasn't afraid, the truth was that I was terrified. I didn't want to die, or be stuck here for years. I also didn't want my family to suffer, and I certainly didn't want to give up anything that might harm them.

It wasn't too long after he left that the sun started to set, and I began to hear it: the screaming. It was nearby, and I knew that it was no mistake that I was hearing it either. The wards on this place were such that sound would only go where they wanted it to. The pained cries of another prisoner were being used to scare me, to make me afraid, to give up what they wanted without a fight. Something I would certainly have done if they came in now.

I hated myself for doing it, but I began to act, poorly.

"This is a great way to make people like you, you know, absolutely great. I mean, I'm feeling much more loyal, certainly. Really, there's no need . . ." One of the guards looked in at me with furrowed brows, but seeing that I was still and standing by the window where I always was, she turned away, letting me rant.

The more I did it, the more I poorly acted, the more my mana began to respond. It was weak, slow, and something I'd only practiced a few times, but it existed, and I only needed a couple of spells.

The iron of the chain around my wrist wasn't very pure. I knew they wanted the secret to making aluminum, sky-metal as they called it, and it gave me a perverse pleasure to use that same technique to escape now. The impurities, and the oxidation of one of the little links moved to two little lines on one of the links, weakening it until it nearly crumbled away. I needed it to hold just a moment while I got the portal up, just in case my wardens looked in while I was setting up my escape.

The harder part came now. I couldn't sing or dance, and those were easier than the stupid ranting I was doing now, but I persisted, looking out the window into the storehouse. Past the broken shutter and into the darkness.

It worked though, slowly and with difficulty, probably due to the much higher distance than I was used to. The portal began to form. First it was a slight shimmering and shaking in the air, then it slowly began to grow, inch by inch. Just a bit bigger and I'd be able to slip through. I bent down to get ready to jump.

"SHUT UP, YOU STUPID!" One of the guards erupted, her eyes appearing in the door. Our gazes briefly met as she saw what I was doing, her eyes widening visibly. "KEYS!"

I'd never stopped my casting, and now I switched to song. Time was something I'd be out of in seconds. While I did so, I yanked, the little chain making a *chink* sound as the corrosion and weakness did its job and popped away.

One of the guards was significantly stronger than the others, and she must have gotten tired of their fumbling. With a kick, the door to my cell buckled and broke. The infuriated soldier stood there, sword in her hand and ready for only an instant before blurring forward.

It was now or never. I dove through the gateway, hoping that it was enough to take me through to the other side. The silver blade seemed to slow as it came forward and I fell back. It seemed she'd not anticipated me passing through the seemingly solid wall, and would miss my neck.

Sadly, I'd brought my left arm up, a desperate reaction to shield myself from the blade.

Time sped back up and everything happened in an instant. The world shifted dizzyingly as I passed through the tunnel in space. Before I realized what had happened, I felt a sharp yanking from my arm and I found myself through, landing hard on some kind of hay or something.

With a thought, I killed the portal spell. Nobody had followed me through yet, but they were sure to in moments. I needed to move, and fast.

It took a second, probably due to the adrenaline, before the pain hit. It came around the same time I noticed all the sticky fluid. My arm, the one I'd raised in defense, flared in agony and I screamed into the bale I'd fallen onto.

Soon as I looked down, I saw it. A few inches below my left elbow there was a clean line, and everything below that was gone. There was also a lot of blood, really a lot of blood, that was coming out of the wound.

I didn't even think, I just started singing. "Auld Lang Syne" wasn't really a thematic song for this—at least I hoped it wouldn't be—but it was absolutely the first thing that popped into my head and I didn't have the time to question it.

The words flowed and flowed, staunching the wound. I got cold; it must have been so much colder out here than in that cell, and I was exhausted. I just wanted to sleep. I needed to finish this though. Get this done, else I would die here.

My vision blurred in the slight light of the moon, but I could still feel the wound seal. I smiled, and promptly passed out.

CHAPTER 15

✦

INTO THE TUNDRA

When I awoke, my head was still spinning. There were bells, such loud bells, sounding continuously. With an idle thought, I reached up to scratch my face. That was when my eyes snapped back open, senses burning as I remembered where I was.

My left hand was gone, my right still had a shackle and a bit of chain dangling from it. I was laying on . . . a brief look confirmed that it was indeed hay. Straw had just a slight difference in texture. Outside, the night was still dark, the bells signaling my escape still going, I couldn't have been out for long. That conclusion was backed by all the blood I was covered in, still sticky and wet.

I needed to go, to either get out of this town, or get to a better hiding spot by morning. Thankfully, all the practice had paid off and I wasn't completely out of mana. As for my hand, it could be fixed with magic. I even knew the spells, though it would take a good long while. The fact that my school had forced that course on me was now a blessing rather than a chore.

My heart was beating fast and my skin cold, but still I tried to rise, a decision I instantly regretted. Soon as my head rose off the makeshift bed, the world shifted and turned, nearly causing me to lose my lunch. My limbs also felt weak as a baby deer.

"Crap, how much blood did I lose?" I whispered, looking down.

While the moonlight drifting in from the ajar window wasn't much, it was enough to see the shiny black puddles all over everything. It was safe to say I'd lost somewhere between "a lot" and "way too damn much" blood. Travel like this would be . . . difficult.

The brief look at the window showed me other things though.

Everywhere lights were on, and soldiers were flooding the streets like angry ants. As for other people, there were none. It was men in armor only, and they were going building to building. That was bad.

I knew that they had people who could, and with all this blood would, sense me. Even at night, even if I was invisible, there was no promise that I'd be able to hide. I could fight . . . but that would only attract attention, which was the last thing I wanted. There was no winning in an open combat; there were too many and too strong opponents.

I began spellcasting quickly: spells to clean the blood, spells to make myself unseen. Even if it wasn't perfect, it might throw some of my enemies off. Even Rooke, the rough professor who'd helped me when I needed it, was my enemy. I'd even have to fight Lief if he came out; that boy who'd once been so kind.

I shook my head. They'd kill or torture me, there was no getting around that. I needed to be able to do the same to them. I hoped it would never come to it, but for now I had other opponents. The soldiers who were going all over the place might have people who could see me in their ranks, and they would be trying to stop me—they were the first hurdle.

I let my eyes shift over everything I could see from my new vantage point as I began to build up magic. I needed to slow them down at least, and I had a few options. The first would be a bubble of silence around myself, then invisibility. I needed points—there were hoardings on the walls, and from this angle I could see the ones right beside the gate. The other direction showed a possible harbor, but the ocean was probably a bad direction to take.

A look up showed a few fliers—some of the mages here must have known how to fly; that was fairly rare. I was already going to be doing some weather magic, so a bit more wouldn't hurt. As my spells built, fog descended upon this city, whose name I didn't even know.

The fliers went wild, like angry hornets as they tried to weave something to dispel my fog. Really, they should have been more concerned about themselves. Only one seemed to realize the danger and started to drop before the first bolt of lightning arced across the sky.

As the hovering forms dropped, I went back to my escape. I found my designated point on the hoardings just before the fog got high enough, and punched a small hole.

"She's somewhere, and active. Teams of two, all of these buildings, quickly, quickly, men!" I heard someone yell from nearby just as I slipped through my portal, leaving a small surprise behind me.

I had to stop when I arrived, if only briefly. I was burning through mana like water through a sieve, and that couldn't keep going on forever. Similarly, I nearly fainted from blood loss and stress. That was okay. My surprise would take a few moments to get going, and I could use that time for a quick breather as I reoriented myself.

As for the fog, I let it drop a bit. If they didn't have someone blow it away, it'd keep for a while, and if they did . . . well, I couldn't spare the mana. It took only a couple of minutes before my present made itself known.

Hay burned, burned almost like paper. The tiny little flame that I'd set off as I was leaving quickly spread through my former resting spot, and before they'd managed to rid the city of fog, an angry red and orange glow was shining from within, visible even through the pea soup.

This would lead to even more panic, and that was good for me. I looked out of the city, and my heart sank. Far as I could see, it looked like nothing but tundra. There were some rocks here and there, but nothing particularly substantial, and no woods that I could slip into. It was going to be a long, hard night.

I took my time to find a flat spot, as far away as I felt comfortable, and made one last portal. After slipping through that, I was out and moving as fast as I could.

Blood loss was a real bitch, but adrenaline was one hell of a drug. While I felt like death, my legs didn't give out. I jogged as quickly as I could, not even caring about the direction, just wanting distance. I needed to be far away and go as quickly as I could; everything else mattered little.

My mana soon began to flag and I had to start dropping spells. First went the sound barrier. If someone was close enough to hear me now, I was probably screwed anyway. I pushed the invisibility for nearly an hour, by which time I should have been little more than a spot on the horizon for the city-folk. Some people might have still been able to see me, but not many.

Eventually my eyes adjusted, and I could see some of the landscape. Most of it was flat, but off in the distance to my left I could see some mountains. The other side had . . . I wasn't sure, but I'd seen a harbor, so my guess was the ocean. I made a slight turn. If nothing else, the rocky cliffs would break the line of sight and perhaps give me some shelter.

I walked and walked until my legs felt like they would give out. The sun made itself known, and gave me a direction for east and some more light. That was a plus and minus. I certainly didn't want to be seen, but now I could see considerably better to choose my path.

The mountains were still far off, but there were now a few rocks sticking up here and there. I made my way over, looking for something that might amount to shelter. It took me several tries, zigzagging a bit as I kept moving toward the far-off sentinels. On my third try, I found one that had a small overhang. It was open on two sides, with little protection, but there were no residents and I was wiped. I crawled in and fell into a deep sleep almost instantly.

I awoke in even more pain somehow. Every inch of me felt frozen, and I realized that I'd fallen asleep in a bleeding tundra without any source of warmth. I was still sore and exhausted, but my mana had at least seen fit to return, and nobody was immediately threatening me. So, that was something.

While I wove up my old warmth spell and checked myself over for frostbite, I started to take stock. I had the prison clothing, which was warm enough but not great, poor shoes, and what was left of my shackle. I was glad that I managed to keep that, since it gave me at least a little metal. Without tools, shaping it into something useful would be really hard, but a knife, even a little one, would be worth the effort.

I sipped water from an ice cup and ate a cheese sandwich I had conjured while doing the first little bit of work on my arm. I really wanted that hand back. The situation was bad, but as long as I could evade whoever they sent after me, it was workable. Based on the geography and temperature, I was probably somewhere in the north, but who even knew where?

I could double back and head for the ocean, but that felt risky. There were a lot more roads near coasts, and if I went near a beach, a passing boat might see me. The odds of that were low, but I couldn't take the chance.

One invisibility spell later, I started on my way out. I alternated between jogging and walking for most of the morning until I found a good spot to break for lunch. The mountains were getting closer and closer but still loomed far away.

I was glad that I took that time to rest, and even picked a big rock to sit on. Otherwise, I wouldn't have seen them.

Behind me was a large group of men. They were still a mile or two out, but were doing a poor job of hiding themselves. I could also clearly see how they were tracking me. At the front were nearly a dozen hounds, noses low as they made their way forward.

"Crap, crap, crap, crap," I said to myself. They surely had plenty of men who could stop me.

When in doubt—teleport. I made a gate, then a series of two more to break my scent trail, and got back on the move as quickly as I could. I'd nearly lost again, and I had no desire to find out what that group wanted.

With invisibility and warming spells up—both of which I now refused to take down—my mana was barely able to recharge. I limited how many gates I was making after the first few but now made it a policy to do so periodically, if for no better reason than to break the scent trail.

This escape was going to take longer than I hoped.

Selene

Locked in a dark cell, I wept, curled up in a small ball of fear. I counted myself lucky. Something had made them stop hurting me. Whatever it was, it currently took all of their attention off me. It had been almost a full day, and still they left me alone—a blessing. The only major change was a guard now stationed in the cell, watching me like a hawk.

With a small noise, the door opened once again, and the foul, snake-looking man came back. He stood in the doorway. This monster was no caster and had no aura, but he still scared me more than any man I'd ever met.

"Ah, Selene, my apologies for the . . . interruption. Where were we . . . hmm, actually, never mind. I have some questions for you. Questions about teleportation."

CHAPTER 16

✦

UP THE MOUNTAINS

Marco

My hands hurt, my legs hurt, the damn hounds were exhausted, and all the men were pissed. Well, most of them at least. The wizard, one of the higher-ups from back home in Ice's End, the once free city, seemed more or less unbothered.

"Sir, we can't keep up like this. From what you'd told us, we should have run the girl to ground in the first couple days, but it's been nearly a week and a half. We don't have supplies, and the men are starting to lose their discipline," I explained, not for the first time.

"Then return it to them. That is your job, is it not?" Rooke, their oft unpleasant leader, said. "Our scouts have seen a few flashes that could have been her, and we're still on the trail. That girl must be captured."

"Because of the teleportation?" I asked. I was no mage, but it seemed like a big deal.

"No, because if she makes it back to civilization and her little empire, she'll bring the whole of it down upon us. We may be strong, but they'll level the city."

"Sir," I tried. "That girl's going up the Glacial Mountains. Chances are she'll die before she gets anywhere near civilized lands, caster or not."

"You don't know her like I do. Get the men, get the hounds, and continue." His tone told me that we were done for now, but nobody was gonna like it.

I returned to the other huntsmen. Most of the hunters in the city had been pulled for this mission, and as the informal leader of most of the parties sent out onto the tundra and hills, I'd been elected spokesman. Honestly, I'd have preferred it if literally anyone else had been chosen to deal with the damn magic users.

"What'd they say?" asked Jacob, one of my cousins.

"What do you think?" I responded, to several sighs.

"We'll have to stop soon, regardless of what they want," Old Man Jenkins observed, rubbing his hand. It was an old injury, broken during one of his many trips out of the city.

"Storm coming, old timer?" Everyone worth their weight knew that old folks had a line on the weather.

"Aye, two days, three at most, and a nasty one it'll be if we get much deeper into the mountains."

"Don't know about you lot, but I've no want to look for some runaway lass in the middle of a blizzard," one of the other men said, trying to get his hounds back up for the morning. The dogs seemed less than interested in the idea.

"Me neither, but you try to turn back and head home, and that wizard might cook you where you stand. We all know what they did to the folk who tried to resist them taking over."

It had been a very sore spot. Lady Astrid, now *Queen* Astrid, had been popular, even if some women had complained about the number of wives her father had. As for old Lord Knud . . . he'd been good at running things, and was fair, regardless of his faults.

Nobody had believed that the previous ruler had died in his sleep, and that his daughter had decided to marry this prince from far-off was also dubious. Those who had tried to fight back though, had been dealt with both quickly and with extreme prejudice. When the fighters had fallen, their homes were even destroyed or taken, leaving their families to the winter without stores or shelter.

Some had taken them in, when they thought they could get away with it. Marco himself had a niece who'd been slipped into his house under the guise of another daughter, at least as far as anyone else was concerned. But when the snows had melted, more than one body had been found buried over the long, cold season. There was an understanding between the common folk and the invaders after that—the newcomers ruled but didn't really care what the commoners did, while the commoners kept the peace and acted like good little servants.

After a few more minutes, the men were ready once again. "All right, lads, let's see if we can finish this up and get home," Marco said as they got back on the trail, knowing they'd lose it another half dozen or so times today.

Alana

My pursuers were . . . driven. I'd been running and hiding for days now, taking them up hills and doubling back, and crossing a few small streams. It didn't seem to bother them and hardly slowed them down. I had no doubt that in an open fight, I'd lose. They'd decidedly brought enough people to take me down, but as the hills turned to small cliffs, my options opened.

I was considering traps and indirect forms of combat that would work, and work well, but might expose me. Simply teleporting up and down and along the cliffs would slow them a lot, though, and maybe get me further out than they could track. The former would more significantly impair, the latter might not work or take too much time to bear fruit.

I frowned, deciding to take a mix of the two. If I found something I could drop on them, I would, but until then I'd just have to make these men hate their lives. Regardless, the rougher the terrain got, the easier a campaign of attrition would become.

I took a break after finding a small cliff to pop up. From here I'd have a slightly better vantage and good eyes on my trail.

"Damn." I sighed as I sat down, seeing my foot. "Guess you were made for being warm on stone floors, not hiking through wilderness, huh?"

I pulled the shoe off, examining the ripped seam. A small spell could fix that well enough, but the whole thing was beginning to wear down. I was glad, though I'd never admit it, that my mother's pressure had led to me learning a few sewing spells, as they were coming in dead useful repairing clothing that had never been designed for its current use.

No matter how you cut it, I was in rough shape. It was cold, very cold, even if my guess was early autumn, but the altitude was making it worse. I dared not light a fire, which would give away my position as quickly as anything, and the nights had been bad. My items were falling apart and so was my body. I was filthy, tired, and only healing had kept the blisters at bay.

Bread and cheese was also not an ideal diet for long periods. During my childhood I'd always been able to scrounge something up, or trade for it, but here I didn't know the plants, and didn't have time to stop. Short breaks between hikes to heal up and eat, or sleep as much as I could, was all I was getting.

The only upside was that I could feel some of my spells getting easier. Teleporting like I was doing wonders for the cost of that particular spell. Healing too, for while I'd known and practiced the basics for most of my life, I was constantly fixing up small aches and pains that in civilization I might have ignored. Couldn't let stuff like that go out here in the wild though, or I'd be dead on my feet even sooner then it looked.

I'd regrown some of my amputated arm, but that was slow going, and would have been so, even with access to proper priests. The nub was still sore, no matter what I did, and there was more than a bit of phantom pain. I wasn't sure what to do about that, other than get on fixing it.

The mountain range, whose name I'd yet to learn, went east southeast, and I'd have abandoned it had it not been a good way to push back on my pursuers. From what I knew, it had been more north to south at the coast, but this turn was not ideal. I didn't know where I was, but based on weather, I was guessing south was where I wanted to head, if only to avoid the cold that seemed to be getting worse by the day.

No time for that right now though. I rose to continue my trek and put as much distance between me and those maniacs as I could.

I ran along the cliff, portaled to one nearby, and then ran along a small ridge for nearly an hour. Most of my day was spent making my way along the edge of a valley and the one beyond it, keeping below the ice-capped mountain nearby.

As the sun began to set, I found a small cave. These were all over the place, and while I'd had to rough it in little more than covers under fallen logs for the last few days, decent shelter was very welcome. It even had a surprise for me; it was warm.

These mountains must have been at least partially volcanic, because there was a small trickle coming from deeper in that was definitely a hot spring. Sadly, it was nowhere near big enough for me to properly wash myself, and it was way too hot, but I'd take what small victories I could get. Even if the whole place had a funky, almost musky odor.

As I picked up a few nearby rushes to form a makeshift bed, snow began to fall. That was unwelcome, as it would both make me easier to follow and be wholly unpleasant to hike through. There was nothing I could do but sigh though.

I ate dinner, same as it had been, and almost instantly fell asleep. Between mana use and plain exertion, I was always at least a little sleepy, and the pleasant warmth all around was unbelievably soothing compared to the chill I'd been saddled with for so long.

When I awoke, it was with a start. It was pitch-black, and there was a powerful howling and chill wind. I didn't know how long I'd been asleep, but it couldn't have been all night, since the sun was still absent, with not even the faintest hint of light showing.

It rankled on my ongoing desire to stay unseen, but eventually I made a small light. Looking toward the cave entrance, I saw little other than a wall of white. The snow that had started had apparently built to a fever pitch. That storm blowing outside my little safe-zone was a monster; complete whiteout conditions, and something that would have made me stay inside for a week.

Could I go out into that mess and survive? Well, maybe. With my magic I could stay warm. If I did though, I doubted I'd be able to navigate jack and might get way off course, or even fall somewhere unpleasant. There was also no assurance that I'd ever find another shelter, much less one that could keep me warm like I was now.

"What about my hunters, though?" I asked myself.

I nearly laughed as I thought about their situation. I was sure that they had at least a few magic users, either casters or physical, and I was guessing at least one bard to supply them. Would they be able to see me in this though? Absolutely not. What about following my trail? I honestly doubted those hounds could find their own tails if they went out in this, and they'd all freeze or use magic like water trying to keep going. It looked like mother nature had decided to give me a bit of rest.

Still smiling, I turned to my shackle. I needed a tool, particularly a knife, and while working the metal would be a right pain with my current state, I could stand to use just a bit of mana on this project. I used the same rusting trick I'd used to break it from its chain to remove it from my wrist, and then got to work.

I was having to ad-lib the spell here, as working metal wasn't my thing. It was possible though, if slow and costly. Bit by bit I shaped the steel, pulling and twisting, trying to get something that even looked right. At home I'd have used tools and would've had a workable blade in only a few minutes, but this was a mess.

I took a few naps between work sessions, and watched as the opening of the cave went from pitch-black to solid white, and now faded back with an almost golden tint. The ability to just relax a bit was doing me wonders, at least emotionally.

My blade was . . . well it was ugly, but it was sharp, and it had a handle . . . ish. My lack of experience was clear here, and I'd need to work on it more when I got the chance, but it was something.

The spell I had made to do this was a sort of mix of heat, kinetic force, and imagining the metal to be like clay. It was messy and I didn't like it, but when I'd started, I was tired and probably not thinking my best. I looked at the result, trying to think of ways I might improve upon the magic.

As I sat there thinking, I heard something loudly approaching the cave. A shadow formed in the blank whiteness, moving toward me. It was big, huge really, and decidedly non-human.

"Oh . . . crap," I said.

CHAPTER 17

✦

OUT OF THE CAVE

The shape in the blinding snow slowly resolved itself as it lumbered into view. The bear stumbled into the mouth of the cave, covered in white powder and looking, for the moment, slightly confused. It was kind of cute, if not significantly larger than I would have hoped to be dealing with right now.

I locked eyes with the newcomer, whose home I might have been invading. Sure, I'd been here a bit longer, but based on the stink that my new friend brought with him, and how it matched so well with what I was dealing with now, he probably stayed here periodically. I really should have guessed that when I'd smelled the place.

The stare down lasted only a few moments. The bear seemed to decide that I was most unwelcome in his abode, having slept in his bed, sat on his chair, and well, there was no porridge, but the feeling held. He reared up on his hind legs and roared. The sound was stunning, making my hair move from where I stood on the warm stone floor.

Unfortunately for him, Mr. Bear had very greatly misunderstood his place. When I stood before his roar rather unfazed, he looked very confused, as if he could see how badly he'd messed up. Then he came down as if to charge at me.

I gave him my own roar in response, a powerful scream without the least bit of restraint. Even as a child I'd been capable of dropping men to their knees and making them bleed from their eyes and ears. This bear was no mage and no magical beast; he didn't even have the slightest bit of an aura. No, Mr. Bear was just a regular, albeit very large ursine.

The scream dropped him like a sack of flour, bawling in pain on the floor of the cave. I then began to weave my spell to take his breath away. It wasn't kind by any means, but I was hungry and in no mood to get mauled by an injured animal. I knew the feeling he was going through, and that it would be terrible for him, but it was the quickest way I could dispatch him without letting loose lightning in this cave—something that seemed a bit risky.

After making sure the animal was dead, I quickly began the cleaning process. I wasn't an expert at this or anything, but I'd been raised in a farm village and had some small quantity of experience. Between my shiny (ugly) new knife and my magic, the process went down without any issues.

I had to destroy the organs. I used fire magic at the mouth of the cave to do it, but it was needed. I'd heard several times that some of the organs, and I couldn't remember which ones, were really bad to eat, and I didn't want to take any risks. Was it the liver or something? I honestly couldn't find the memory clearly enough, so I just trashed the lot. I could have tossed them outside, but the risk of any more visitors discouraged that.

While the meat—and *boy* was there a ton—tasted great, the real boon was the skin. Drying it was a bit of a mess, as was getting all the little bits of flesh off. But once that was done, I had a new bedroll slash cloak, and more than enough left over to do some outfit repairs. If I ever got back to civilization, I'd have to hide how useful sewing magic was, or my mother would be smug until she died and probably force me into other similar pursuits.

Then I waited, and waited, and waited. This storm seemed endless, never letting up and never slowing down. There was an onslaught of snow for days, piling up near everything except my little cave entrance. The hot trickle of water was more than enough to keep it at bay, and I was quite glad for that small mercy. I could see some trees that were gosh knows how deep in the white mess.

Twice did the snow around my cave fall, covering the opening. I used what fire and heat I dared, and between that and my happy little stream, it was quickly cleared away. It never stopped falling though. Getting through this was going to be a disaster.

I turned back toward the rushes that had served as my bed and then as the drying rack for the bear skin. I had a new use for them now and one I hoped they would serve well in. If they failed . . . I'd have to figure something new out, but who knew what that would be. I knew I had no experience with anything like skiing, which would have been a real boon here.

After nearly a week of snow, the storm finally ceased, leaving behind a bright white field. Trees that weren't fully buried were partially so, and the whole mountain range looked like someone had dipped it in frosting. Into this new landscape I waddled, improvised snow shoes on my feet and a pack on my back. Things were not good, but I had to wonder if the men sent after me were having a worse time.

Rooke

This may have been the worst couple weeks I'd experienced in quite some time. They even rivaled the period when the capital fell. During that time, I'd been at more risk and certainly lost more than I had so far, but it was nowhere near so personally unpleasant. The last few years had been hard, but they had hardened me. I would weather this too.

The blizzard, which was finally clearing, was one monster of a storm. If I hadn't seen it in action, I might have thought it was magical in nature. No, the storm was natural, displaying none of the telltale signs that someone had summoned it—something to look out for when you're following a weather mage.

Pulling up the stone to form a shelter had been easy enough. As was heating it, so long as the casters took shifts. The commoners mostly relied on their beasts to keep them warm, huddled up in piles. While it may have smelled, and looked completely ludicrous, they all seemed to be warmer than I was most of the time, even with magical heat.

Those same commoners looked to be on the edge of revolt. I could see how they were looking at the rest of us, their anger and fear at this mission. None had moved to do anything yet, but I had little doubt that if we didn't find our target soon, an example would be made of someone. Food had kept them satisfied through the storm, but none of them were happy with the current state of things, and it was all too obvious that they wanted nothing more than to turn around and go home—not that I could really blame them.

The bard I brought along for healing and food, things we might well need, had been working beyond all expectations. His magic was feeding our whole expedition, aided only by a few light supplies we'd brought. It was taking most of what he could do, but that was fine; he was more than worth the effort of calling him to join and would be even more so if we could capture Alana.

I hoped to still capture the girl. I'd watched over her for years, and while she was not my child, she was one of my favorites. I'd enjoyed teaching, but only once in a while did I meet someone who was truly worth the effort, and she certainly had been. Even more so now with her teleportation. That alone was a legendary magic, and if I could just convince her . . .

"Storm's fading, sir. We should move out soon," a member of my team said.

"Yes, get the trackers. Can they even follow her after all this?" As I looked at him, I saw one of the leaders of the huntsmen nearby and let my eyes drift over to him.

"Snow will mess with the scent a good bit, sir, but once we find the trail, following it should be easier. Do you think she survived? Many a good man have died to a storm like that one," the hunter said as he scratched his chin.

"She survived. That girl is nothing if not good at keeping herself alive in bad situations."

"You know her well then?"

"Yes," I said, which was all the answer he needed.

In my mind I reached out, calling out to her. Alana just needed to come back. If she did so on her own, I could help her. It could be like old times, only better. She could help me with my research, and I with hers, and together we could build magic to rival anything in history. She'd come so far, and learned so incredibly much, but she needed to bend the knee; if she just would. The boy, Lief, would spare her. They'd met, and he was kind.

Yet everything I knew told me she'd keep running. If what I'd seen were right, she'd likely fight when we caught up to her too. Could I take her alive? Well, I had brought a healer to aid in that goal. It was a hard hope, since any fight between us would be one losing power that could easily kill. I'd try to preserve her life, but honestly it would be an uphill battle, as would returning her back to the city. Teleportation would be worth the effort though, as I doubted the other girl could do it properly, else she would have already.

"Are we ready then?" I asked after a few minutes. The men had their things packed.

"Aye," came the response from several directions.

"Then let us go."

CHAPTER 18

◆

IT'S A . . .

The cliffs kept getting bigger and more imposing by the day. That was only good for me, though I tried to keep an eye on the areas outside of the mountains, skirting where I could, rather than trying to see just how deep I could go. Mostly I didn't think anyone would be building here, but if I could get to civilization, I might find help.

I had no delusions that I would definitely find someone allied if I did find a settlement, but even an unallied city would be a great help. I needed supplies, aid, roads, and any help in travel I could get. If I were lucky, I might find somewhere that was part of the empire, but even if it was some city-state or something, I might still find a road or route home. Even in the worst case I would be able to disappear into a crowd.

As a bard, I didn't really have the best offensive or defensive options, but solo travel wasn't the worst. My magic covered most of my basic needs with ease. Optimally I'd have been with a group that could help cover my weaknesses, but we had to deal with the world we had, not the world we wanted to have.

I kept travelling, mostly in an eastward direction, for the next three days, every now and then taking a look behind me to see if my pursuit continued. On the fourth day, I saw them coming along a ridge I'd passed the day before. A series of tiny dots slipping down the mountainside. That was unfortunate, but I knew where they were, and where they were coming from. Now I just needed a plan.

If my enemies hadn't been sent home by that storm, they were prepared to follow me till the end of the world, and I just couldn't have that.

They had more casters, and more experienced people. Eventually they'd catch up and then I'd lose, unless I could beat them somehow.

It took me another day to find the right spot. I quickly marched up to the sheer cliff, the easiest approach clear. The snow there was cleared out as if some wildlife had been using the path over the last few days to ascend and descend. The path itself was small, a crack between the two sides of the cliff, perhaps ten feet wide, that snaked upwards in an odd way.

This place looked like it would be a heavily used trail for game and the like, but I saw none around—odd. I'd seen a few deer, and the aurochs that were everywhere in the north, but not much else. Predators who were smart avoided humans, and those that were magical were rare in comparison.

"A stream?" I wondered as I approached the little path, seeing the windswept ice all around the opening.

Sure enough, it was. What looked to me like a pathway was instead the spot where a stream had cut through the cliff and flowed down into a small pond at the base. How interesting. The next interesting thing was the pattern in the ice. I was careful as I teleported around it, before dragging part of my bearskin across it ever so gently. I didn't want to walk on that and was very glad to the kindly soldier who'd shown it to me.

Once I reached the top, I sang up a small snowstorm to hide what I'd seen, then began my preparations in earnest.

Marco

I was tired, the hounds were tired, the men were tired. None of us cared about this stupid girl, none of us wanted to cross these fucking mountains. We all just wanted to go home.

The men had been getting more and more angry by the day, almost by the hour. This hunt had gone on for far, far too long, and there was no way we'd be paid enough when it finally ended to justify all the time. Our families needed the food we brought back, or the coin. What were these damn nobles thinking.

Cousin Jacob, in particular, was livid. He had a wife and daughters. They needed him, not some runaway little girl. He'd been keeping it low-key, but soon enough I wouldn't be able to stop him from doing something stupid. If there weren't so many of the nobles with us, someone already would have, and damn the consequences.

There were just over a dozen of us, and five of the mages. Two wizards and two knights that I could see, along with a bard. The last of which was definitely favored by the lads. He'd helped us at every turn, even cleaning up some of the aches and pains that just came with something like this. Had he not been with the rest of the group, we'd all be raising cups to the man when we got back.

"You doing all right, old timer?" I asked Old Man Jenkins as I slipped back beside him, letting my hounds slow in their tracking.

"Ain't cut out for this anymore, boy. If not for the singin' lad, I'd've lost fingers last night. The cold is getting to me, slow but sure."

I reached over to take his shoulder. "Don't worry, friend, we'll be headed home soon enough." I didn't know if it were true or not, but it was the best I could do.

The path the girl had taken was painfully obvious. There was only one way up this cliff, and every man with eyes could see it.

"I suppose we know what way she went then," one of the knights said, moving forward.

"Aye, sir, that's the way," I replied as the nobles began to move forward.

They joined up with us hunters near the front as we moved. The path was tight, but we'd want a few of them to lead out, in case of a trap. If they lost the hounds, they might as well have lost every chance of tracking their runaway.

Before we reached the opening, I stopped and looked down, squinting for a moment.

"What is it?" asked Rooke, the leader of this abominable expedition.

"It didn't snow last night, did it?" I replied.

The man paled and looked up, screaming, "TRAP!!! IT'S A TRAP. EVERYONE B—"

Before he finished, there was a flash of actinic blue above us and the sound of explosion. A bolt of lightning had struck the cliff, sending up a wave of steam before there was an ominous crack and the rock above began to fall. It looked like a mountain plummeting down from above.

The wizards were quick to toss shields of force up and stick shattering lances out, breaking the wall of stone that fell near them. I heard the pained cries of the men and their dogs, as the onslaught of boulders big as housecats crushed them.

A wave of wind passed, kicking up the snow, and I saw her. The girl we'd been chasing was so close, right there before us. She was young, and beautiful. Her eyes, surrounded by tired circles, were the color of sapphires and ablaze with fury. Her hair was a pale blonde, blowing behind her in the wind she'd made. Though her clothes were ragged, and she seemed to be missing a hand, she turned beautifully in some kind of dance.

The angry knights didn't hesitate and charged their target, not intending to let her escape. Their feet, heavy in their boots, pounded on the ice.

"NO, YOU FOOLS!" Rooke howled, but it was too late.

A second bolt landed right where the girl was, just as two men struck out their swords, which passed straight through her. The image of the girl disappeared in the flash that left the two knights struggling to pick themselves off the ground. While the strike had knocked them off their feet, their armor glowed brightly, seeming to absorb almost all of the attack. Guess they'd come prepared.

"Fall in! We need to find where she is, we need—" Our leader tried to take control of the situation, only to be interrupted by an odd keening noise and a loud cracking.

Tentacles shot upwards from the ice, grabbing at the knights. They'd been lured into place. I paled at all the odd occurrences, but reflex took over and I let out a loud cry. "Ice Grasper, home!" The last part was a call for all the hounds to fall back; one of several common commands hunters trained into all our dogs.

The recognition also got me to turn and run. That was a magic beast, and one none of us could deal with. The wizards seemed stunned and hissed in anger, but they had bigger problems.

The creature was slamming the two armored men around like a child smacking her doll against a table. Had they been ready for it, perhaps they'd have made short work of it, but they were stunned by the bolt, and the beast was livid at the pain from the attacks made upon it. The casters surged forward, spells slicing limbs to free their companions.

Soon enough, the beast was defeated. One of the two knights had been killed, his head slammed against a rock hard enough that even his armor and superhuman strength couldn't help him survive. The other was badly injured. The bard began to tend to his broken bones quickly but had to take a break after only a few minutes. Rooke pulled the kind caster away to have a word with him while the knight rested and caught his breath.

The other wizard marched up to us. We'd lost three hunters. Another two were hurt bad and would probably die soon. We'd also lost half the hounds, which was enough to threaten our livelihoods. The wizard didn't seem to care, though, and he came right up to us, rage on his face.

"Why didn't you help against the beast!? Sir Grenwald might have survived!" He waved an accusing hand.

Old Man Jenkins was nearest him and spoke, "We don't have weapons to fight something like that, you fool!" He was tired and angry; we all were.

The wizard looked ready to spit blood at his insolence and backhanded him hard, sending the old man to the ground, where he shook like he was having a seizure. The wizard was a fool, and his action sent a wave of hostility through the remaining hunters. My cousin was the first to move, plunging his hunting knife into the man's gut.

Things happened fast. Someone roared in rage, and all of us understood. We'd be killed to a man if this ever got back to the city, so it could never get back. One of the men sent the remaining hounds after the downed knight, a few with longer blades moving forward to aid them. The rest of us charged toward the shocked wizard. Perhaps the bard would be spared if he didn't fight.

Alana

I sat on my cliff behind the men, watching the chaos. I wanted to roll with laughter. Everything had gone better than I could have ever hoped, as mana-intensive as it had been. Their forces had been cut down slightly, several important-looking men falling to the monster.

Right as I was getting ready to make my way off, they started fighting amongst themselves. There must have been some division, because the bastards fell upon their own people. I wanted to cheer; all I needed was a good seat and popcorn. Could I make popcorn? Probably—questions for later. It was a bit dark, but I couldn't bring myself to care too much, at least not right now.

Sadly, before long, one of them opened fire on the crowd. I didn't bother watching how it ended; it didn't matter.

Instead, I turned to the makeshift sled I'd been working on—it was mostly just a log with stripped bark and a bit of shaping—and began my way down the mountainside. This slope looked the right angle for me to give this a go, and I wanted distance fast. Teleporting would be down for the rest of the day with all the mana I'd burnt through, but I had a distinct feeling my enemies would be a bit busy in the meantime.

"Wheeee," I whispered softly as I slid across the snow. I was still worried about being heard, but couldn't resist.

✦

CHAPTER 19

RACE TO THE MEET

Day after day I marched, teleported, and even made a few more sleds, to cover as much ground as I could. I was not going back, and they couldn't make me. It was working too. A week after I'd led my attack on the hunters, I stood on a low mountain slope, looking out on the horizon.

There was smoke, lots of it. If I had to guess, it was perhaps a day's travel away, but I could see the clouds drifting up. I decided to take a chance on something that I'd been thinking about for the last several days, and brought my hands up before me. The space bent, not to teleport, but for a new purpose.

A telescopic lens began to form. The zoom was . . . poor, but it was enough to see the source of the smoke. Buried in a valley beyond some hills stood a small town. *Civilization!* I was saved!

It would still take me at least a day, perhaps two, to get there. From this side there were no roads, but that mattered little. I just needed to make it to the compound.

It only took a few moments to check my gear and begin my descent. I was still pretty well-off, aside from getting low on meat, but that was something easy to fix. All I needed was an inn or a tavern, or really any public place where I could regroup and get some new gear.

There was no time to waste, so as soon as I was ready, I hurried down the mountain, renewed by hope and the joy of things to come.

Marco

I looked up at the mountain so far above, exhausted.

"Which way?" the gruff voice behind me asked.

"Right," I replied, letting the hounds take us to the girl's path.

There were only four of us now, and a few of the hounds. My friends and kinfolk had died screaming, and now it was just me. There were rope marks on my hands, and scars where burns had been quickly mended. I was going to die, that much I knew.

After a few more hours, we finally stopped for lunch.

"How far behind are we?" asked Rooke, his voice cold.

"A day, maybe two."

"Good, then we're catching up. Remember what I told you."

"I remember," I said, tired. "You'll spare them, then?"

"I swore to it, didn't I? Your family and those of the other traitors will be spared, but only if we return with Alana." I could hear the anger as he said it, still furious at our betrayal.

"Right after you cut my head off?"

"You'll get one last chance to see your kin, and I'll get another good example to show those who think they can get away with such foolish things. And if you tell the people how foolish you were, I might even give them a bit of food."

I wanted to curse and spit. I wanted to slap the look of contempt right off the bastard's face. He thought he could force us to help him, drag hardworking men out on this stupid mission, and why? Because he was a noble, a mage—what a whoreson. My men and I never wanted for anything other than to live our lives in peace. But him and his people came and stepped all over it. They could all go freeze to death for all I cared.

But I did care about my wife, and the children, and the wives and children of all the others. I was going to die, but if I caught this girl, perhaps they wouldn't. Perhaps I could do one last thing and save them, at least some of them.

Then again, I almost hoped that this Alana girl would just kill all of us in another avalanche or something. I'd die a thousand deaths to see Rooke and his men suffer, and if none of us returned home then there was no chance they'd go after our families.

Durin

I looked down at my desk, tired. These last few weeks had been nearly as tiring as when I'd taken over. The assault on our portal team was still unsolved, several city-states clearly needed to be put in their place, and finally, my son was sick. It was bad enough that even my dear Sophia had stayed behind to keep an eye on him.

I looked up from my desk to see her now, holding our infant boy swaddled against her chest. I couldn't see it, but I knew waves of healing mana were being gently pushed into the small body there, aiding his recovery as best she could.

"He's asleep," she said, her eyes meeting mine.

"That's good. How is he otherwise?"

"You know. And you know what the priests said. It's one of the noble illnesses. It will come again."

I sighed. There was little else to be said. Both of us had been born to high-ranking families, so this wasn't completely unexpected. People of our status almost only ever married people of similar status, and there were so very few of us. The priests understood why this was bad, sometimes disastrous for bloodlines, but it still happened. We'd been told that our son, and potentially other children, should we have any, would suffer from afflictions such as this.

There was no real cure. At least, not in the normal way. Normal disease was simple; a bard or priest could fix it in moments, even if some of the symptoms lasted a few days more. Those were only a threat to the poor, who couldn't afford treatment, or were last in line when things spread too quickly.

However, this was in our blood. It couldn't be taken from him, for it was as much a part of him as his hands or feet. They of course would treat the symptoms, but there was no end. He would suffer, again and again. I knew this, understood it, but screamed inside because I knew there was nothing I could do.

"When it's safe, we'll take him to Linden. There are stories of some of the elder priests fixing even these maladies, and they will for us, my love." I rose and moved beside her, wrapping one arm around her shoulders.

"I know, I know. Though I hate the idea of my son around those child snatchers."

I smiled indulgently, knowing my dear's opinion on how the orders claimed every child who showed priest abilities. Our son hadn't, but he clearly had an aura of some kind, so it was a worry that they might want him to join should his power manifest in that way. Not that she'd have any of it.

"They won't take him." I kissed her cheek before turning to leave the room. "Sadly, I must go back to work."

The schedule from my desk showed all the places I had to be over the next ten days. An appearance in the capital, another in Lithere, and there was also a team going out to set up a portal at a site they'd found, a forward base and vacationing spot. The last one seemed silly, but I did want to get a look at what they were thinking. After that, I needed to inspect the army being sent east.

One of those city-states had taken my people, and all of them would suffer for the insult of attacking my diplomats. This couldn't be allowed to slide; not only was a certain general enraged, but letting them get away with this would only teach others this was acceptable. I would crush them and retrieve my people, and nobody else would dare take such actions again.

Alana

The ground flew by beneath me, and though I'd avoided teleporting too much, I was still making excellent time. In just a few hours I'd be there, safe and sound. My feet thumped hard against the snow-covered ground as I made my way to the valley lip, step-by-step until I finally reached the top and got a look at my destination.

I laughed and laughed, falling to my knees with tears streaming down my face. Tears that continued even after the laughing stopped. This had to be some kind of sick joke.

CHAPTER 20

✦

HOT SPRING BATTLE

It was the valley from before—where I'd tested the portals. The smoke was not smoke at all, rather the steam from the many hot springs laced throughout, drifting upward in billowing plumes. I wasn't sure if I should curse, or laugh, or weep at the sheer irony. There was one thing I knew for certain though: I knew which way to go to get home, and that was worth cheering for. If any of those men had kept up their chase, they'd be in for a real surprise when Durin's people fell upon them like wolves on a carcass.

As soon as I managed to break into the heated bathhouse, I found a good spot and passed out.

Dras's attempt at making a spa was dumb, but beggars couldn't be choosers, and I'd soon be headed somewhere I knew I could be safe. The benches here may have been unpadded stone, but they were certainly better than nothing.

The next morning, I made my way to one of the heated pools. A few spells cleaned out the small mess that had made its way into the steaming water, and I slipped in. The liquid warmed my bones and calmed the aches of travel as I relaxed and let myself drift a bit. Someone had even been so kind as to leave behind a bit of soap, which was promptly used to scrub layers of filth from my skin and hair.

I even took the time to do a quick wash on my clothes. I had a cleaning spell, but it behaved oddly on a lot of things. Floors and walls and other hard things were no problem, but on skin, it stripped the hair and left everything feeling a bit dry, and on clothing it had a tendency to damage the cloth over time. Between that and my self-imposed restrictions on mana use, I'd ended up smelling something awful.

The missing hand was still bothering me something fierce. I'd managed to keep rebuilding down the arm and would have eventually fixed it up, but the sheer unusualness of trying to move around without both hands was jarring me still. Time after time I reached up to grab something, only to realize that I couldn't, and I still felt like there was something there, my mind not yet accepting the configuration of my body.

I didn't know how long I stayed in the bath, but eventually I had to leave. I needed to continue on, regardless of how much I wanted to stay. I still had people after me, and just collapsing here would not do. So I rose, dried everything off with magic, and began the process of packing to leave. If I hurried, it wouldn't be much longer before I was back at Durin's fortress. I could relax after that.

As I pulled my pack on and took a bite of the last bit of bear meat, I heard a noise. There was an explosive crash, followed by the sounds of shouting. In an instant, my blood turned to freezing ice, numbing me to my core. Surely I hadn't taken that long? Would my enemies have already caught up? I spun invisibility around myself and prepared to fight or flee, depending on what I saw when I left, then I headed for the door.

Captain Omar

I never really thought I'd be back in this place. After our stop during the testing of those new gates, I did have to admit it was nice, but it was still rather secluded. Though if you really wanted somewhere where the researchers and soldiers from your secret ice base could relax, I suppose it fit the bill quite nicely.

As I stood, one of the new gate models fresh from production was being put up. The pair of wizards setting it up was now under much heavier guard after reports of an assault on one of these teams. It was an easy enough job keeping an eye on them while they did their work. I'd been told in no uncertain way that these two didn't know how to make more gates, they were just here for setup, but I was still to kill them if it looked like they may get captured.

At the least, they were making a quick job of it. We'd only been here for an hour or two, and they were already finalizing the basic protections. Before noon, we'd be ready to call for an inspection. If rumors were to be believed, someone major wanted to give this place a look themselves, one of the generals or someone.

Rooke

By midafternoon, we'd crested the mountain and were looking for where in the world my erstwhile former student had run off to. Our last living knight, Sir Leonard, turned, hissing.

"You see something?" I asked, concerned. The last time we'd missed something important, a lot of men had died.

"Smoke, lots of it. Wait, no, steam?" He looked confused, his gaze narrowing at the clouds in front of us.

"Smoke or steam? It could be important."

"Steam, and movement—lots of it, and people. Sir, she'll have gone, and we need to move fast."

I turned to what was left of our group. "Fall in, everyone. I'm going to cast a rather big spell. Sir Leonard, find the girl quickly, and kill anyone who gets in the way." I looked at our bard. "Kaleb, take out everyone you can using screams, low burst. We need to disable fast. Other than that, I'll leave it to you." He nodded. Finally, I set my eyes on the traitor. "Stay out of our way, keep the hounds close to you; interfere and you'll suffer."

I was not as powerful as Grandfather, but it mattered little. I spun magic out from myself in the same manner as his escape spell. Around us a ball formed of light and a purest force, cushioning us as we sped off. The whole thing was mana intense, but there was little time to worry if we were to capture her.

I struggled to keep the magic in place as we flew through the air like a stone from a sling. This was the fastest I could go, but I hesitated to use travel at this speed because of the difficulty and danger. They would know when we arrived.

Through the slight yellow haze of the magic, I saw the mass of men pouring out around some central square and aimed to one side. I needed to take as many of them out as possible while still giving us good firing lines, and this was it. I'd have to depend on the shield's power as we landed, but it would be enough. These people appeared to be some kind of military formation, with a man coming down the center, some leader. I'd want to take him out, but that would put us surrounded by all his men, and that was a fool's move.

"Make ready for the king!" It was a shame I couldn't share my insights with the others in time. They were good, though, and I could depend on their abilities.

We struck with an explosive force, and in a credit to training, all came out ready to fight. Kaleb roared power into the crowd of surprised soldiers while I followed with a wave of force.

As my second spell blew away the dust, I saw something which both excited me and sent a thrill of worry up my spine. Standing still in the center of the square, surrounded by the men we'd blitzed to the ground, was a figure I hadn't expected.

"My, my, what an entrance," the false emperor said calmly as he brushed dust from his pitch-black cloak. On either side of him, a pair of guards had taken up defensive stances.

I smirked at him, false confidence flaring. "Well, I was coming for a troublesome escapee, but to find the arch-traitor himself, how wonderful."

"Take them," Durin said to his men, and the battle began.

Alana

I made a short-range teleport out the building's door, covered in every defense I could manage and hidden well from sight. As the first light hit my eyes, the ongoing battle spread into view. Everywhere around were men of the empire, their black armor striking against the light dusting of snow on the ground. Many were down, many dead, but near the center the fighting was fierce.

It was three on five, but that didn't mean the fight was easy. I saw Rooke, slinging spell after spell, beside him a knight with a great sword flashing in the sun, and if I had to guess from the scream attacks, it was a bard. Opposing them were four men I didn't know, a caster of some kind and three armored knights, all formed around . . . Emperor Durin?

While they may have been outnumbered, Rooke's men were giving a magnificent showing. The casters slung attacks while the knight blocked the approach of opposing warriors. The bard's attacks may not have been too effective against his enemies, but he did enough to push back and distract the opposing guards, letting the knight hold his ground. Rooke was their big gun, though, and threw spell after spell at Durin, enough that his own caster was struggling to keep them from the emperor.

I began to sing, for I knew which side I was on. It took a few moments to process and begin the spinning up of magic, and in that time I watched two of Durin's guardians fall to the knight's blade. The bardic support was enough to throw them off at critical moments, something I filed away for later.

The bard was my first target, and I used my new attack spell. As he drew in breath for another scream, one to throw the last guard and perhaps distract Durin himself, he gasped. The man looked like his eyes would bulge from his head as a hand went to his throat, trying to find what was sweeping his breath from his lungs.

The knight moved to engage Emperor Durin, having not yet realized his support was gone. I'd never seen Durin fight, but he advanced without fear, having gained a two-hander of his own from somewhere. The two clashed steel, and in an instant, it became clear that the knight was out of his league.

"Hit him!" he screamed at the bard, not knowing that the man had fallen to his knees and was clawing at his throat. An instant later, the knight's neck met the emperor's blade and found itself detached from its head.

While this happened, my former teacher proved that he was more than skilled enough to instruct others on magic. Durin's caster finally had his many shields and spells fail and was sent careening into a nearby stone building, where he crunched against the wall and fell motionless to the cold ground.

I was too busy with the bard, the concentration to defeat him with a very new spell too much for me to struggle with another spell at the moment. He'd realized it was a spell and was pushing as hard as he could against it to resist, something I'd never had to deal with before. As I feared he might shake it off, a ragged-looking man stepped in, impaling the bard with a spear he'd taken from one of the many fallen soldiers.

Durin

I didn't know what was going on, but that wizard indicated he was after someone. It could wait. For now, I needed to survive this battle.

To one side, a peasant-looking fellow was trying to kill that damnable bard. Something else was going on there though. From the corner of my eye, I could see the man had already been struggling against some invisible foe . . .

Oh, this might be good, but only if I could make it through. I'd already activated my emergency items, and soon enough, backup would be here.

I recognized the mage I was up against, and that was bad. I hadn't seen him in decades, but he came from one of the most honored of families, and they were honored for a reason.

"Hello, Rooke, an honor to do battle with you," I said.

"Shut up, bastard. Once you're dead, nothing else will matter." As he spoke, some spell formed between his hands, a hateful, brilliant red light pouring from what looked to be a firestorm compressed into a small ball.

As if I'd let him. I pushed with my feet and shot forward like an arrow from a bow to cut him down before he could launch that destructive blast.

There was a feeling like striking a wall of steel, and I bounced. He must have put some kind of shield up; that was bad. With my armor and defensive items . . . it was not enough, nowhere near enough for a direct hit from a duke-level wizard. My brain, so used to battlefields, struggled to find some route of escape.

With a sneer of victory, Rooke loosed his spell, the projectile arcing toward me like a miniature sun. Before it could hit, the air shimmered. A small circle appeared before me, swallowing the magic like the horizon overtaking the brilliant ball it so closely resembled.

An instant later, not even a blink, and the light from Rooke's spell reappeared right beside him. It struck, bathing the world in brilliant light as it detonated against the wizard. I was thrown like a rag doll, laughing the whole way.

While I tried to catch my breath, I heard the fast pattering of feet against the hard ground. "Shit, shit, be alive, please be alive." I didn't open my eyes until the feminine voice got closer, leaning over me and beginning to sing. For a moment, I let her spell happen and felt the healing flow gently into my tired, but mostly uninjured, flesh.

There was so much to consider in that moment. This girl had clearly saved my life, even at risk to herself. She'd taken down my enemies, and unless I was very mistaken, that last spell was a cast portal, something nobody I knew of could do—magic of legend. In the past I worried that she'd had secrets, and clearly that was so, but she was also clearly with me. I could kill her and remove any fear of what she could become, or I could bring her closer. A risk, but I was never one to shy from a risk.

As I slowly slid my eyes open, I took a look at her. She was clean, but . . . rough. Her dress was that of a prisoner, thin and now worn ragged, patched in places with some kind of animal fur, her face tired and a bit sunken from bad diet.

I gave the kindest smile I could. "There you are, Alana. We've been looking all over for you," I said, trying to sound weaker than I felt.

"I imagine so. It's been a bad time, a really bad time."

I slowly sat up and tried to register everything else. One thing stuck out at me. "Your hand . . ."

"Lost it when I escaped—long story." I imagined someone's head would be ripped off by her father after he heard that.

"Tell me later, child. For now, my men are hurt, can you help them?" I nodded toward the many injured soldiers.

"Of course," she said as she turned to them and got to work.

Out of the corner of my eye I saw a man looking at us as he struggled to pick himself up from the ground. This was the one who'd killed the enemy bard, and I went over to him to ascertain his motivations. As I approached, the man knelt, like the peasants had before my ascension when any high noble gave them audience.

"I mean you no ill, sir. These men, the ones who attacked you took my city. They killed our people, so many of our people, sir. They'd have killed me too."

Sometimes one could do a good deed while achieving their aims, so I gently smiled and placed a hand on his shoulder. "Rise, my friend. You saved my life; tell me of your home. Let us go and save your people, together."

I knew from the look in his eyes that those few words had bought me this man's loyalty, and when I did free his city, it would be eternal.

Alana

It took hours to go over my story in full, but I didn't complain. The interviewer was a kindly-looking old scribe who spoke to me very sparingly as we sat in the dining hall. He asked me to go over the story and wrote notes as I spoke. I did notice him making some points to clarify things here and there on the paper.

Father arrived about halfway through, and after hugging me, sat down nearby. He seemed to have a lot he wanted to say, but he held his tongue for the moment and let the debrief continue.

"I used a variant of the portals in a spell form to redirect Rooke's attack, and it killed him. After a bit of cleanup, we returned here," I finished.

"Thank you. I do have a few questions, things that need clarification, if you don't mind too much." The scribe looked up from his paper.

"Certainly."

"Let us start with the most important question. Did you happen to see your compatriot, Selene? I would assume she was in the same prison, but confirmation would be useful."

My stomach dropped. "She was taken?"

"Yes," the old man said.

"I-I didn't realize . . . I heard screaming in the prison after I was awoken, but I didn't know . . . I didn't know they were torturing her." I let the last bit hang, unwilling to think about it, about that horrible sound coming from her. "I left her." I could feel the blood leaving my skin as I said it.

"We're going to get her back," Father said, placing his hand on my shoulder. "We're going to go there and kill those bastards and get her back."

I looked over and saw the look in his eyes. I'd seen him angry, and I'd seen him when he was taking command. What I saw now was a black hatred, and even though it wasn't directed at me, I still felt afraid of him in that moment.

"To that end, dear, we need to know everything you do about this town. The name and location would be a good place to start, as well as anything you can remember about the people there or the layout of the prison." The scribe seemed to want to bring me back to the task at hand, the task I could help with most immediately.

"I never heard a name, and I didn't see much of the prison."

I spent the next several hours repeating everything I could remember, and drawing poor maps where I could. They wanted the details I knew, but some were coming from the man brought in by Emperor Durin. He'd also been getting debriefed, but somewhere else.

I spent three days in recovery while things came together. The fortress was alive with action as teams were being brought in and moved about for the impending attack on Ice's End. They were drilling, and making sure that they all knew their part in the plan before the battle. I spent most of this time trying to teach another bard how to use the portal spell, without being able to explain space-time in any manner that would make sense without a lot of background.

When he finally managed to make a portal, I was reminded of my own first attempt, except it was even poorer. The poor guy made a portal the size of a quarter that left a smear across the room as he passed out. It was sad, because my understanding was that he had a massive amount of mana.

I was high on the mana front, but by no means the highest in the kingdom. Most of my ability was the simple fact that I specialized far more than the average bard. While they could do more than I could, I could do what I did best; a trade-off, but one that I was quite happy with.

"Hmm, not sure what happened here. You might try going through the setup portals to get a feel for it, or it might just take practice." I put a reassuring hand on the bard's shoulder.

"Oh come on, that was just sad. Something is really wrong," he said, pointing at the smear that was still slowly disappearing.

"Not much worse than my first try. I got one about the size of an apple before I fell over. Had a monster of a headache too." They hadn't asked about when or where I'd first developed this, since I was willing to take on a student.

He sighed. "I think it's the visualization, then. The idea of all the area between as something like stretchy pudding is just weird."

"Mmm," I said sagely. "Nothing for it but practice, then. Maybe get on the portal-building team? Not sure if that would help a bard, but you can try it if you can get permission."

We had to use a bard of course, because the wizard they'd sent to try and learn the technique had utterly failed. He'd spent hours grilling me for information I just didn't know or wouldn't give, and then spent more in meditation only to end up with a headache and a failed spell. There was discussion that this might be an exclusive bardic magic, since I could clearly do it, and a new student was brought in.

I liked the idea of teaching, but teaching this grated. I knew a lot more than I could comfortably tell them, and so it was like holding myself back. I wasn't just watching this man struggle, but letting it happen knowing that I could help him overcome his issues.

Eventually I looked down at my hand. The lost one was still slow in coming back, and I was missing fingers even now. A priest would have been optimal for this kind of work, but there weren't any here. This place was still a secret, and since no priest associated with any army or nation, we couldn't bring them in. Eventually that secrecy would fail to some degree, since a lot of people now knew about it, but it was being maintained for as long as it could be.

After the treatment, I returned to my rooms to get ready for my afternoon. There were a few letters that Dad had seen fit to bring me the day after my return. A pair from Ulanion, the first dated to when I was supposed to return, asking me to contact him at my convenience. The second was dated a few days later once the information of the kidnapping had been made public, and said much the same, along with a hope that it would reach me in good health. There was also one from work that had been sent while I was still away, asking me to have a written report ready when I returned.

Dad had expected I would demand to return home as soon as possible, but I had other plans. I didn't know if there were spies in Lithere or whether they would try to take me hostage again. If that was true, then the idea of me going back there, or even letting too many people know that I had made it back, was a bad idea. So I'd requested to stay at the fortress for the time being. That request had been met with quick approval by both my father and the staff responsible for the fortress.

My other requests were not as easy. Mother had to be told that I was safe, but wouldn't be coming home. I wished my father good luck on that one. I also requested Ulanion to be moved to the fortress for the time being. I wanted someone for company, and with all the soldiers being moved around, this shouldn't be an issue. If nothing else, they could write him off as being assigned by Father as my bodyguard or something. That had led to a lot of displeasure on Father's part, but he'd let it happen. He and my brother were both going to be attacking Ice's End, and if something happened here while a large part of Durin's forces were otherwise occupied, skilled archers would be a boon.

The knock on my door came just after noon.

"Why, hello there," I said to the familiar Elven man as I opened the door.

"You know," he said. "I was not expecting you to order me here because you needed an, ahem, bodyguard and boyfriend to help you."

"You did ask me to contact you at my earliest convenience, did you not?" I asked.

"Fair enough and it is good to see you." He smiled and shook his head.

I looked him over briefly and found that he was much the same as he had been. He looked a little more comfortable in the less formal version of military garb but other than that was still himself. I also noticed he had a thin book with him.

He passed his gaze over me, as well, but zeroed in on my hand.

"Things did not go according to plan," I explained.

"Are you okay?" he asked, looking concerned.

"I will be. I found a room we can use to talk. It's nice, and has a lovely view of the gardens."

We walked quietly. The whole place was busy, and while the halls weren't crowded, it seemed best not to disturb others. Soon enough, we reached our destination and I led the way in.

"Okay, why is there such a big, empty room here?" he asked as he looked around the place. It was huge, and had windows all along the inner side that looked down on the green courtyard.

"This place wasn't designed as a fortress," I told him.

"Really?" He looked surprised by that.

"Well, not just a fortress. It was supposed to be a school. This would probably have been one of the classrooms."

He took a while to process that. "The portals then . . ."

"To bring students here and return them home would be my guess," I explained.

"I would have loved to have seen such a place."

"Me too, but I still like it as it is. Emperor Durin may not be perfect, but he's doing a lot of good, really a lot." I shrugged and changed the subject. "But enough about that, what's with the book?"

He chuckled. "Well, I knew I couldn't trade letters with you for a while, so I made you something." He put down the little volume and opened it to the first page.

I recognized it immediately; it was Lithere, as seen from the high end of the main street in some kind of charcoal. It looked down on the skyline, and you could make out many of the city's major buildings. It looked almost like a photo.

"You drew this?"

"I thought you might like to see the city as I did, and I took up a bit of sketching so I could show people what I saw when I was scouting. It's not the work of an expert or anything, but I thought you might like it." He smiled nervously, and I was reminded once again how elves had a very skewed idea of what skilled meant.

I carefully flipped a few more pages. The school, a market, a scene of a sunrise that I heavily suspected was from the restaurant where he'd taken me to breakfast.

"I love it," I said quietly. "Thank you. This is something right out of that . . ." I didn't really have the right words.

"Do you wish to talk about it?" he asked.

"Let's sit."

There were a few benches pushed back against one wall, and we settled on one. I began, haltingly at first, and skipped the beginning, but I talked. I talked and talked, letting the words flow without worrying about how accurate they were, or if someone could get the information they needed; I just let loose. My feelings and fears, my hopes, the terror when I realized I'd been captured, the savage glee as I watched my trap close upon the men trying to hunt me down.

He listened to all of it. He didn't interrupt, or ask questions, or seek clarification, he just listened. One arm wrapped around me, and loosely he held me as I spilled my story. The few times I stopped, I saw his eyes focused on me, his attention to it all. Once I'd finished he just sat there, waiting for me to be ready.

"What do you think?" I finally asked, after having sat still for a long while.

"That there are some men I'd really like to kill. Sadly, I have a more important job to take care of at the moment."

I pulled myself up and kissed him. It just felt right.

CHAPTER 22

✦

OPENING MOVES

The next few days were actually pleasant. Other than some light paperwork—I was milking the missing fingers to escape what I could—and my few lessons with the other bard, I was mostly free to do as I pleased. I either spent time seeing Ulanion or hurrying along my hand. The former was a distraction from the latter.

My fingers were growing back at an extremely fast rate, but there were still practical concerns. I was physically strained, slightly malnourished, and the process took an intense amount of energy. Unless I was willing to commit to a rather insane dietary plan, I would need to take things slow. While it *could* be done faster, that would only lead to problems down the road.

My boyfriend, as I had now accepted him as such, had guard duty and a few minor tasks of his own, but still managed to spend time with me. We couldn't really do much, or go anywhere, but we could chat. He even sketched me a couple of times in various places throughout the castle, sitting by a window or walking through the courtyard. There was care taken to omit any militarily relevant details from any of those.

He asked me about the people we were up against, and I told him what I could. I told him the names I knew, and the appearances, and what they were like. I even told him how it was a bit odd, because I'd met the leader of this enemy force many, many years ago when we were both children. Ulanion listened closely as I told him of the undercity and our adventure there, and how Lief had come off as so kind. He also sat in deep attention when I described their spymaster and the fear he instilled in me with his snake-like face.

Around the time the soldiers moved out en masse, I received a letter. Rooke had been a wanted man who was an enemy of the state and had a sizable bounty on his head. A large quantity of gold had been allocated to me for my service in stopping him. It felt . . . dirty, the money for killing someone who I'd once had such a close relationship with. Rooke had been my mentor and guardian, and while I'd done my best to forget about how I was responsible for his death, I was indeed. I satisfied myself with the knowledge that had I not acted, not only would Durin be dead, but I would probably be getting tortured right now; it still felt sickening though.

Verren, Expeditionary Force to Ice's End

After a couple of long weeks, we were nearing the end of this journey, but there were problems. There always were with any operation, but these were worse than average, and I personally wanted none of the rats to escape our assault. Perhaps we'd been spoiled with the absolute victory we'd managed again and again, and now struggled against an enemy we couldn't so easily abuse.

The main problem we were having was that there were absolutely no gates anywhere near the city. When the network had first been built, it had apparently not been considered important enough to warrant one, if it had even existed. By our standards, the city was only middling in size, and very, very far from anything of great note. The only reason it hadn't been forcibly annexed by someone else earlier was that it was just too far from anything else.

The general plan was to use the mountains to close in without being seen, then swing around and down from the north side. Getting warships up here would take weeks longer than we had, and would alert our enemies; the same reason we wanted to avoid the coast to the city's south. There was a chance that we'd get found out, but that was viewed as very minor.

Once we got close enough, a team was going to enter by posing as the hunting party those bastards had sent after my daughter. Their goal would be to get inside the walls and set up a gate we'd brought. From there we could quickly move our strongest people into the city and begin taking it. Resistance from the civilians was expected to be near zero, and some might even help us.

The problem with the plan was that there was a good chance that the infiltration would fail, or the gate would be destroyed before enough of our people were in. In either of those cases, we'd need to move fast to break into the city walls and begin taking down the nobles who'd hidden here. Time was not on our side, since if Selene broke, or was moved away, one of our strongest weapons could fall into our enemy's hands.

I sighed as we entered the final stretch, looking down at the maps we'd managed to cobble together.

"Something wrong, Father?" John asked. He looked more like I had at his age by the day.

"It's a mess, we need more time, but we don't have it. The men are also unhappy about the orders concerning the wizard girl." I couldn't bring myself to say her name, not until we had her safe.

"None of us like them, but we all know it must be as it is." He winced as he thought about our orders. "We'll get her back though; our best are being sent in."

"I know they'll do what they must, but I can't help but think of how I would be if it were your sister."

We stared at each other for a long moment. Our orders were clear, and everyone understood it. If Selene couldn't be brought back to us, she was to be executed. There was no room for leeway there. If at any point we failed and it seemed like she might fall back into their hands, the soldiers were to kill her without hesitation.

"It won't come to that," my son said, trying to convince himself as much as it was for me.

"No, it won't. Your team and mine will be the ones attacking the prison. Look here." I pulled over the map and went through our angles of approach with him, and where we were to strike.

Marco

The day had finally come, and I was ready for it. While a lot of the soldiers had insisted that only those capable of magic should be in the forward team, they couldn't deny me. I knew the city and its routes better than anyone. I would be here as we pierced the gate and made our way inside, and I would see to it that we succeeded in kicking these haughty monsters out of my home.

My team, as it was, had been carefully chosen. We needed people who could fake—at least at a distance—the look of those who'd gone out hunting the bard girl, so choices were a bit limited. The biggest of the limits, though, was that everyone involved had to be able to hide their aura like it wasn't there, not that I really understood what that meant. Apparently, casters had some way of identifying those who could use magic, but the traces could be hidden, something like that.

Other than the weird magic stuff, we had to make sure the clothes looked right and provide enough hounds that were close enough to our own that the guards wouldn't question it. I dreaded the idea that some of them would be killed for opening the city gate to us, but there was no way around it. We needed in, and enough time for the gate, a folding contraption hidden in bundles like it was our target, to be set up.

Snow crunched under my feet as we approached the gate, and I let my eyes roam. Something seemed slightly off, but I couldn't place my finger on it. I gave another hard look toward the wall and squinted.

"Something's wrong, cousin," I said to the man beside me. He was in the guise of my now dead kinsman.

"Hm?"

"Less gate guards than normal, and I don't see the captain anywhere."

We'd been warned to try and keep conversation as casual and normal as possible. It seemed silly, but one of the soldiers told me they had men with senses that would boggle my mind, and we had to assume our enemy did too.

"I'll tell the wizard. He should know what to do," he said.

My heart was thundering in my chest as we came nearer and nearer. I was no soldier, just a man trying to do the best he could for his people. If this was a trap, or if something was wrong, I'd have to depend on these with me. I didn't know if they could stand up to whatever might be thrown at us, but I'd just have to trust them.

The gates opened at our approach; we were expected after all. In an instant, it all came to a head.

Soon as we stepped in, one of the guards came down. He was in a hurry, it seemed, and looked at us only briefly.

"Sirs, we're so glad to see you. There's been a bit of worry that you were so slow to return, and I'm told His Majesty wants a report as soon as possible," the man said. "We sent a runner to the castle as soon as we saw you. They should be sending someone down promptly."

As he spoke, a woman on horseback sped toward us. She was yelling from beneath her cloak. "Oh, thank goodness . . ."

Her eyes landed on the man impersonating the dead wizard, and I could see the shock for only a moment. Before she could say anything else, the impersonator's hand flicked up and a lance of fire speared the rider's head, taking it clean off. The gate guards looked shocked as soldiers revealed themselves and began the attack in earnest.

✦

CHAPTER 23

BATTLE OF ICE'S END

Verren

I waited, looking between the gate in front of me and the city so far away. We'd seen our team make it to the gates, but it would be up to them once they were inside the city. If they failed, we would have to act immediately to push against the city's walls. That would be a waste of life and time, time that we might well need if we were to retrieve young Selene alive and whole.

With a pop, the gate came alive and there was an explosion of action. Teams One and Two had already been lined up and charged, and our fastest warriors sped like arrows loosed through the portal to the other side. Within seconds, a small flare was thrown over the wall to our side.

"Safe, go!" one of the observers shouted.

The world sped as my team blasted forward, my son's not far behind. There was the briefest odd sensation as I passed the glowing barrier and exited into a scene of carnage. The team that had punctured the defenses was still in the process of bringing down the soldiers who hadn't fallen in the initial strike, but I had no time to waste.

The key to this operation would be speed. We needed to hit hard and fast enough that there was no chance for response. Our goals were to secure the girl, kill the would-be king, and take the city, in that order, and I aimed to achieve them. The more time we had until we were found out the better, but I doubted we could pull it off before they found out.

Stones flew below my feet as I sped down the main road. My men were at my back, and before me were only the innocent peasants who we had no issue with, so I didn't need to slow my pace at all as they stepped aside to let us pass. Eventually we took to the roofs to speed our way up as we approached the small castle overlooking the town. Like black streaks we flew across the city, able to speed our way forward.

Before we'd reached the wall I would be aiming for, there was a flash of red light across the sky and a booming explosion coming from somewhere behind us near the wall. As soon as it went up others quickly followed, and before me I could see several above the castle being sent skyward—a warning to all that we were coming.

Spells began to rain outward from the castle, but they were slow and lesser versions of what I was expecting. We knew that Lief had escaped with nearly a hundred magic users of various sorts, and had been potentially joined by others. Some of those who'd managed to escape were, like the man Emperor Durin had fought, highly ranked in society and magically powerful to match. Power tended to run in families, and these were old ones, skilled and strong. The lack of potent attacks made no sense.

My eyes flowed forward and around, looking for the issue, looking for the trap. Our enemy was far too weak and I needed to know why. The men lost when they'd blown up one of their previous bases came to the forefront of my mind, and I signaled my men. I had to grit my teeth as we slowed just below the prison cells.

"We need a mage here to look for traps, now. Contact the other teams, nobody goes in until we're sure it's clear." My men nodded and sent up flares of their own.

It would take minutes, precious minutes to get someone to look for what we were after, but we couldn't take the risk. If the building was set up to destroy itself, we couldn't risk it. A failure here would be a failure of the whole operation, and that couldn't happen.

While I waited, I heard a voice boom across the city. "People of Ice's End, do not panic, we mean you no harm. We have come to destroy the invaders who have damaged your city and killed so many innocents. Please stay out of the way, retreat to your homes if you can. The Empire of Shadows is no enemy of yours." That was standard protocol at this point, and our good reputation did wonders for keeping civilian resistance down.

One of the wizards finally made it to me, a team covering his approach with spells aimed at the defenders inside.

"Sir, what do you need?" he asked.

"To know if this place is going to explode, and a new entrance; I'm not taking any of the standard ones."

With a quick jerk of his head, he began casting, a small light spreading out from his hands and into the stone of the building. It moved quickly through and into the edifice, working like water flowing down a stream.

"There are enchantments all over it, but I can't tell what they do. I'll start breaking them, sir."

Cracks started to appear in the stone, nothing but hairline fractures. This was the most effective way to disable enchantments on a building, at least partially. If you could get close enough, you could damage the physical structure of any item, and this would damage the magic powering it. It wouldn't be enough to stop every enchantment, and it wouldn't stop things that produced certain fields, but it would have to do.

Before too long, the sound of screaming echoed around us.

"HELP, HELP I'M IN HERE!!!" The panicked screams of the trapped girl sounded through the wall. She must have been enhancing the sound somehow. It was followed up with a series of explosions.

"Door, now!" I called to our wizard, pointing. Their wards keeping the sound contained must have failed, and it sounded like she was already fighting.

There was a good reason enemy casters were seldom imprisoned, or if they were, they were treated quite well. It was almost impossible to hold a caster long-term. It could be done, and you could abuse them until they were afraid to fight back, but if they ever saw a chance, they could always cast again. Wards could only do so much, and it was often better to simply get them to stay by telling them that they would be treated well if they behaved, and killed if they resisted. The fools had fought the old way and were now learning why it had held so long.

By the time a hole had been ripped through the stone wall, things had deteriorated for both sides. As I entered the hallway, I could see the various spells arcing from one of the nearby cells. Guards were scattered about, some clearly injured from the frantic casting of the captive wizard.

From the cell emerged the form of a large man in full armor. The runes covering it glowed as the struggling form he was holding by the neck did all she could to escape. Selene had some kind of shield covering most of her body, and fire and electricity shot from her hands. Below the magic she looked ragged, with matted hair, sunken features, and a dress that was ripped and torn to pieces. She kicked and clawed and spat angrily, but in the few seconds that passed as my enemy and I locked eyes, her mouth moved like a fish out of water. He wanted her alive, and unconscious.

We both wanted her to survive, so I waited the few moments. I had backup coming and I doubted he did, so now that I had eyes on the girl, I just needed to keep them there. He drew his sword and we kept staring before he dropped her, now silent and breathing small breaths in a lump on the floor. That was ideal; her being in the middle of this fight would only complicate an already problematic battle.

"You may call me Lord Fallon," the man declared.

"General Verren. I've heard of you," I responded.

"And I you. This should be enjoyable."

We launched at each other at the same time. His shorter sword twisted like a snake as I stabbed in again and again. While he wasn't as fast as I was, the larger angles from which he could bring his weapon to bear down were a strong advantage, as was his armor. Normally, I relied on my speed and agility to make strong strikes before retreating. In an open field I would have had the advantage, and even with the hall I wasn't out of tricks, but it limited me to mostly parries and stabs.

Our weapons clashed again and again. He swung a third time and I pushed the blade to the side, only to return with a powerful thrust. He dodged, the point of my spear skidding against his breastplate, runes igniting along the surface. Both our sets of gear were enchanted, and heavily so. His heavy armor could block blows for a time, but my much lighter set allowed me to easily dodge his slashes.

I suddenly lost my footing, and he was able to close. As the man forced his way into my guard, I choked up on my weapon, grabbing just below the blade. I had one chance and aimed up into his armpit, stabbing for the opening in the armor with all I had as he brought his weapon up for a killing blow.

There was an audible *clang* as the point of my spear impacted a small shield that sprung to life, the enchantment on his armor covering the weakness. I looked up in defiance as I saw him start to move again.

Before he could bring his sword down, though, there was a flash of silver and a ringing as something impacted it, throwing the angle and destroying the blow. Then there was a second flash lower down, aiming at another weak point in the armor. John had arrived, and below his helmet I could see the rage on his face. In the heat of the battle, neither of us had seen his unit breaking through the far wall.

Whereas my weapon had been poorly suited for this fight, John's weapons were perfect. His twin blades were between daggers and swords and curved forward like the extended claws of a large cat, batting our opponent this way and that. One made to intercept Lord Fallon's sword while the other darted forward, trying to find a weakness in the shielding the formidable enchanted metal provided.

The battle turned with the two of us now against his one. There was more fighting around us, but nobody wanted to close on our clash. The moments my son bought me gave me time to reset, and his pressure gave me openings I hadn't had before. Blades clashed and we finally began to land our shots.

I nearly shouted with joy as a hard thrust pierced into the back of the armored man's knee, sending out a small spray of blood. The knight turned his attention back my way, bringing his blade down, where I met it with the haft of my own armament. John didn't let him have a moment of respite and began making his own attacks in the same spot, soon sending the man to one knee.

"Surrender and you will be shown mercy," I commanded.

The man growled and swung one last time, hurling himself forward toward the still form of Selene, seeking to deprive us of our target and the important intelligence she might provide. John intercepted his blade again, the sword bouncing away less than an inch from the broken woman's neck.

Now on the floor, he had little defense as both of us fell upon him, holding him in place while I drove my spearpoint into the gap of his visor. It took long seconds to shatter the barrier there as the man struggled, only for the blade to enter his eye and end his life. Not once did he call for mercy, or offer to yield, which was a shame, I'd heard of him, and heard he was a good man, but here he was merely my enemy.

CHAPTER 24

✦

FALLEN CITY

Selene

I awoke with a start, finding myself lying on the ground, men bustling all around me. I wasn't chained, or held, or even being guarded by a number of soldiers. For a few seconds I looked about in a brief panic. Was I dead? Was this what death was like? Then I saw the color of all the clothes of the soldiers rushing around—all were in darkest black.

As I broke down in tears a man rushed up, kneeling beside the blanket I found beneath me. "Sorry, miss, bit of a rush. Are you hurt?" he asked.

"Am I safe?" I responded, looking at him.

"Yes, miss, of course. Sorry that I don't know you, but one of the forward teams just brought you in. You're not from Ice's End, are you?" I could see the knowledge dawning on him.

"No," I responded.

"You're Selene, aren't you?" Understanding bloomed on his face.

"Yes." It was a bit scary that he knew my name.

"Well, Emperor Durin will be pleased. One of our main missions was to save you, miss. To save you and liberate these people." He pointed, and I looked at the city in the distance. There was fighting still going on, but fires burned near the center at what looked like a large castle.

I let loose then, weeping continuously. Time flowed away like water as the tears fell. The medic stayed with me, letting me go and letting me hold him when I needed. Eventually I could cry no more, and I saw that night had fallen, and luckily there were blessedly few in the same area as me, and they were all being attended to by men like the one sitting here.

When I was done, I lay back down and slept peacefully for the first time in so long. The darkness only showed me swirling lights and light, kind voices.

Verren

After sending John back with the girl, we continued on, cutting our way through paltry resistance. Room by room we cleared the castle, killing all who resisted. Many of the soldiers I met had no mana, or very little, and after the first push through the strongest, they all threw down their weapons.

It was easy to forget that many men were pressed into service by the nobility in the past. They seemed to have continued here, forcing people to work for them in some capacity or other. I had also been called to war against my will once, and so I knew the look in their eyes that told me they just wanted to go back to their homes and families. The ones I could let live, I did.

Eventually we'd made our way to the heart of the fortress, and as far as we could tell, had it surrounded on all sides. There was some form of barrier over the door, and a number of men were working on disabling it.

"Strong one, General," one of them said as I approached. "We can bust it, but they'll know."

"Put up shields and be prepared for anything. Once it's open and we're clear, we go in," I told him, and the mages nodded, forming up their spells.

Minute after minute passed as they pounded on the barrier, slowly, carefully cracking the turtle's shell. There was no secret here, just the assurance that they had enough firepower to at some point destroy the barrier, and the willingness to wait for the spell to fall. This was no simple ward locked by the stone that held it, but rather some kind of emanation. It went on for what seemed like hours, until cracks like those on the shell of an egg began to form.

From there, it didn't take much longer until the barrier fell, the door behind it exploding inwards. The wooden projectile was torn from its hinges and flung like a toy across the room, landing near the center.

Men flooded in as soon as no trap became apparent, only to find an empty room. Rich carpets lined the floor of the barren chamber. At its center stood the one thing that I had hoped least to find here. A gate had been erected, standing alone, the exit that the rats had used to flee.

"Get some of our specialists here. If they're smart, they've destroyed or disabled the other side, but we need to check regardless." It was likely that they'd want Alana to come and see this, but if it could be managed, I'd have Dras or one of his apprentices come instead. The young man needed to prove himself, and this was a good opportunity for it.

There was nothing more I needed to do after setting down orders and sending my men to it. So I did the same thing I always did after taking a city. There would be reports, and interrogations, and prisoners to deal with, but for now I needed to secure the city and try to minimize casualties from doing it.

I walked back through the streets. It was good to see with one's own eyes the way of things. The stone roads were mostly empty, scared faces peeking out of windows as the soldiers passed this way and that, wondering what would become of them now that a new army had taken over. That was less than ideal, but to know what the status of things were, I needed to see some of the people. So I kept walking, kept looking for someone out and about.

A pair of guards accompanied me, but I paid them no mind as I moved through the streets. The enemy was gone, and my men knew their duty, knew the plan that was in place. I moved deeper and deeper through the alleys, getting a feel for the place, seeking the people. Soon enough I found some.

In a corner behind some storage buildings stood an old shack, at some point used for tools, but long since abandoned, or so it seemed. Outside the door were the clear footsteps coming and going, and they were recent. The windows were broken out, and there was no chimney, but there were eyes looking at me from the darkness as I approached. With a hand signal, my guards moved to cover the other directions.

"I know you're in there," I commanded. "Come out."

The door cracked and a girl appeared. Her clothes were ragged and too small. Her face was pinched tight and her eyes sunken, sad, broken, dying. It was a face I knew all too well, it was the face my son had described seeing on the people of their former village. Someone, a boy probably, was pulling at her from the side, trying to get her to come back to the safety of the little shack. She pushed him away and came into full view.

"Please." That was all she said as she faced me, fear reverberating through her voice.

"I'm not here to hurt you, girl. How many are with you in there?" I asked. At her hesitation I added, "I will have it searched shortly, so don't lie."

I could see her teeth clench. She was probably the oldest here, around age fifteen or so. "Six," she finally said.

"How many have you lost since the others took this city?" I responded.

"Forty-seven," she said. I could see how that pained her.

That number was high, way too high. There were probably around ten-or-so thousand people in this city total.

"Why so many?" I asked her.

"If your parents fought against His Majesty. . ." Her expression softened, but her fists still clenched in hatred. "Then after they were killed, your house would be destroyed."

That matched what I knew of the former Bergond nobility, and with what the informant had told us. There didn't appear to be any temple in this town for these kids to have fled to. We were out at the very edge of the world, and their reach was limited—one of the reasons that this place had been chosen, in all likelihood.

"He's gone. Get the kids and bring them." She hesitated, so I clarified, "I'm getting you all food and taking you somewhere warm to sleep."

The group did not include any young babies or toddlers. There was no way they would have survived. Even still, these children looked scared as my men searched the house and then walked with us down the street. She hadn't lied to me about how many she had, which was a good mark for her. I wouldn't have been too mad if she had, but still appreciated the honesty.

Eventually I found what looked like a tavern of sorts. There were no inns here, as they didn't get many visitors, but it would do. The proprietor looked like he was expecting death when I beat on his door, but upon having a few coins shoved in his hands and being told to get food and blankets, he calmed considerably.

While most of the kids tore into the food the man had procured, I pulled the girl to the side. "This isn't free. I've got a job for you."

"Of course," she said, looking resigned. Perhaps she'd been expecting something, probably something terrible for what they were getting.

"You and those kids are gonna go make rounds to the people you know, and you're gonna tell them what happened here." She looked up in confusion. "Everyone is scared, kid, and scared people do stupid things. I want you and those kids to go and tell them we're not here to pillage, or rape, or wreck things. That's the cost of this. We'll get an orphanage, or send you kids off to one somewhere else soon enough if you've got nowhere to go, but for now I need you to do this."

"But why?" she asked.

"I could tell them, but they won't believe me. So I want you to tell them. Tell them what I did here, tell them what it cost you, tell them that we're not here to hurt them. That's for tomorrow though. For tonight, go and eat." I waved her off to the place where the other kids were, where her own food sat waiting.

Making arrangements with the tavern keeper wasn't hard. Invasions killed his business, and my coin was still gold, even if he didn't recognize the minting. That and a few vague threats about how unhappy I would be if I should find the kids mistreated set things right for now. This had worked in city after city to calm panicking populaces many times, and I had confidence it would work here too.

CHAPTER 25

✦

GATES

Alana

Father had sent in a request for Dras to come and look at the gate they'd found. That was stupid, and all of the people in the gate project agreed on it. Sure, I had no desire to go back to Ice's End, particularly after they'd failed to finish the job properly, but I was nearby, as much as that mattered, and not currently engaged. I was also the best at building these things and really wanted to know what Selene had given them.

Selene hadn't yet come back to Durin's fortress. There were no gates at Ice's End as of yet, and all communication was still through our magic radios. Those were nearing the maximum of their workable limits, regardless of how much we all tried to make it work. We were now only able to communicate at night, for reasons mysterious to everyone.

The original army that had assaulted Ice's End had only one portal pair due to the simple fact that they were still in production, and had used it for infiltration. It was a risky call, but they'd felt it was the right one if they wanted to get in quickly. Sure, it meant that they couldn't get reinforcements or easily retreat here, but the desire had been to crack the city as fast as possible, and they'd done that well, if reports were to be believed.

Finding out that Lief and his merry men had managed to get a portal network of their own had caused some panic among the upper ranks of the empire. There'd been a constant stream of people in and out as Durin mobilized basically everyone to figure out what the implications were.

A team with a gate—the newest one off of Dras's production line— had been dispatched to set up a portal at Ice's End as quickly as they possibly could. Until then, I was cooling my heels and diving deep into any commands that might stop a gate from forming. The latter project hadn't borne a bud, much less a fruit, but we'd see what we could find as time went on.

I was more than a bit surprised when I got a letter requesting me to join the meeting I found myself attending on this bright afternoon, but I was an expert on these gates, and I was present.

"Welcome, Alana, please come in," Durin said as I was led into the meeting room, motioning to a chair near the edge of the large table he sat at.

There were around a dozen old men and women of various persuasions seated. A few were younger, fifty or so perhaps, a few looked like they might blow away in a stiff wind, but I was by far the youngest person here. I recognized only a few from various events over the years, them and Mystien, who'd taken a place near the emperor.

One member of the gathering, a man with greying blonde hair and dark eyes, looked to our leader and at the nod of confirmation, began.

"Thank you for joining us, please call me General Lukas. We have precious few people who understand the portals, and even Mystien here believes you'd be the best one to speak to on this. If reports are to be believed, we have a major problem, but one that leads to a number of questions we need answers to," he said.

I was happy Mystien was trusting me here. He may have been a terrifyingly powerful wizard, and the master of all things water, but portals were my wheelhouse. He might have been able to tell them some things, but this gave me a chance to shine.

"I've several of my own, but I'm afraid that until I see the work, or talk to Selene, I'm unlikely to have all the answers. We sent a request for the rune sequence she used, but the communications have just been too broken for it to come through properly." I frowned slightly; there really was a lot I needed here.

"Well, any general questions then? Like how they made the portal pair so quickly?" he asked.

"I don't know. I imagine they had to make some changes somewhere, but what and where are unclear. Though I think they were probably torturing her to make her work faster, but that's just a guess," I said.

"Can they make more of them?" he tried.

"Doubtful, they didn't have the stone we've been using to upgrade the core." There was a collective sigh of relief at that answer. I knew for a fact that it was possible for one of us to do a setup to upgrade someone after we'd gotten our own; Justin had told me as much.

"What about tracking where they went, or stopping them from working, can you do that?" a nervous-looking woman inquired.

"No on both accounts. I've been looking into options for the last couple of days, something I should have thought of before, but there's nothing yet. I think it might be possible to do, but I'm not even sure on that account." There were a plethora of issues trying to lock down space, if the magic could even do that, and the few thoughts I had didn't have any good method of implementation.

There were a few more questions, but most of them were either really basic, or boiled down to "I'll need to look at this portal first" for answers. This gathering was in all likelihood a panel of the most powerful people on the continent, but that didn't mean they knew everything. Eventually they petered out, moving on to discussing things like how to improve security and what they should be on the lookout for.

"Are they using movable portals like ours?" one of the gathered men asked me, hoping to get an idea of what to tell his men to keep an eye out for. At my deadpan look, he answered himself, "You won't know until you've seen it, right."

When it was time for everyone to leave, Durin asked me to stay behind. Mystien stayed as well, along with a few bodyguards nearby.

"Alana, I would like to know what you view as the worst-case for this," he asked once most of the people had left.

"I can't do the really big things, so I don't know the limits of what he could shove through that portal. It could be bad, but I think Mystien would be the one to ask about that kind of war magic. Depending on where he could get it, and how much mana he could supply, he might be able to do something like drop rocks from really high, or drain a lake somewhere new. Don't know if he'd think to try that though."

Mystien began to furiously scribble. I'd apparently given him some idea, probably bad for some poor bastard years down the line. "Rocks from really high? Not sure how useful that would be," he muttered.

"Do not underestimate the power of gravity," I responded.

I doubted he could manage full-on orbital bombardment, but a big rock from half a mile up was still a force to be reckoned with.

"I want a full report on this after you've had a chance to investigate. Until then, take this." Emperor Durin slid a paper across the table to me.

It took me a full minute to read over it. As I did so, I nearly felt my eyes pop out of my head. It was a writ that gave me the power to act with his authority for the purposes of my investigation. I could demand any resource, or command any troop save the personal retinue of some of the higher authorities of the empire. Even then, it indicated there might be someone doling out consequences if one of those few did decide not to aid me. It was signed and sealed by Durin himself.

"This is . . . a lot of . . ." I babbled.

"Don't use it unless you have to, but I want this done, and done right. You saved my life while killing one of your mentors, Alana, I trust that you will not abuse this freedom." His tone indicated that his trust would still be monitored. I'd rather not have to pull this thing out, but it would help get the job done.

"Thank you," I said softly.

"Think nothing of it. Gather the resources you need, and go."

Two days later, word came in that the gate-delivery team had reached their destination and checks had begun. These would take a bit of time, but soon we were ready to go. I had a dozen guards who'd been picked by Ulanion or myself, and some basic gear. My hope was that we'd be able to get the sequences from Selene quickly and be done with this.

The portal was ready for us when we arrived. Half of my squad went through, with Ulanion popping back to inform me that we had a safe path. I walked up to the glowing plane and stepped forward.

The other side brought me out into some kind of stone building. There were soldiers running about and a general air of business everywhere. It didn't take long to orient myself—military outposts did always organize themselves in the same general manner—and head for the entrance. My brother met me as I approached.

"Hello, little sister," he said as he walked forward.

"What, no Dad?" I replied.

"Dealing with some issues with the town. I assume you want to see it?"

"What I'm here for, John."

He chuckled and led me forward. We seemed to be inside one of the larger halls, or someplace where Lief had taken up residence, so it wasn't a far walk. Before I knew it, I arrived at a heavily guarded room, and with a quick nod from John we were all let through. He wasn't a general or anything, but everyone knew he was an officer, and knew why we were here.

The first thing I thought when I saw the gate was that it appeared very plain. The second thing didn't occur to me until I got almost right up to it.

"What the fuck," I said as I looked around it. There was a place for a power supply, one of the standard ones, but that had been removed. There were also things in the doorway itself to prevent outside activation—all good practices.

"What the actual fuck," I repeated as I looked at the gate itself.

"Something interesting?" John asked, following my gaze.

"This thing's a freaking hazard." I was stunned.

"To us presently?" Ulanion asked, moving to my side and looking about for danger.

"No, to anyone going through it. You'd have to be insane to use this thing. We may need to break it, just in case."

"Um . . . what do you mean, Alana?" John asked.

"There's only one sequence on the whole damn thing, and I don't think it's a fake with the real one hidden. It just says to connect point A to point B, and defining the area, that's it! This is just wrong, dangerously wrong. Has anyone tried to activate it?" I asked.

"One of our wizards tried and failed . . . we figured they'd cut the power or something on the other side, or buried it or whatever," my brother replied.

"Yeah, none of that would work. There's nothing telling it not to connect. It's probably broken, and we should break it. Fuck, Selene was not doing these guys any favors."

"Er . . ." John really could be dense, but the others were looking at me weird too.

"There's no wards, no safeties, there's not even an on switch, or . . . like almost all of what is on ours."

"So it's easy to use?" John asked.

"It's like stringing a rope bridge between two-hundred-foot-tall towers and not installing any sort of guard or handhold. Sure, it works, but if anything slips up even a bit . . . I need to see Selene, now." John looked at me, blinking for a second before I walked up and lightly bonked his forehead with my fist. "Now, John."

CHAPTER 26

◆

THE BROKEN CITY

First things first, I needed to talk to Selene, and I needed her reports. Those had been put to the side for the moment, but that was going to change in a hurry. I rushed toward the door, dragging my brother along for the ride. Then I stopped and looked back at Ulanion.

"Break it. That's the only way we can be sure it can't be reactivated."

He didn't even hesitate as he turned toward the gate, taking a war hammer off one of the guards, who'd had them just in case. I forgot sometimes just how strong he and other physical users were, but it only took him a couple of hits to crack the magical item. Sadly, that was the only way to make sure it never activated again, and with the clearly missing safeguards, I wouldn't have it doing so.

"Alana! Are you insane!?" John exclaimed as the bits of stone crumbled and fell. "You can't just destroy that! It's a captured piece of enemy artifice!"

"You'll find I can. I need to investigate what they have, and that thing potentially activating would stop that." While it was a stretch, I was sure the emperor wouldn't mind too much. Sure, I destroyed it, but the danger to all of us made that menace to magical craft more dangerous than useful. "First, I want to look over what you've gotten from Selene, then we'll go see her."

John looked stunned that I was giving him orders, but complied. I was sure that he would be going on about it later, but for now he knew why I was here, and that he needed to help me get on with it. He led the way back to the makeshift headquarters and found me a side room where I could go over the paperwork.

They'd not gotten much information out of Selene, but they had managed to get her to write down the rune sequence. I ran it over and was glad that she'd provided exactly what was on the gates. She'd also told us that she'd made them only three pairs total. That was impressive feet-dragging, even to me. The other two pairs were smaller. It was a system so that Pair Two was just small enough to fit through Pair One, and Pair Three would barely fit through Pair Two. They'd not gotten out unfolding gates at least, one of the few good notes of today.

I pretended to rub my temples while I retreated into my core. There, I opened up the debugging menu and tossed in Selene's sequence. It came back telling me that it would work just fine, no obvious failure points, because of course it would. The damn thing could be written on my palm, but confirmation was nice. I was a bit surprised that it also came back with a warning that there were no controls added in, and the item would default to on if powered, off if not, until that was done. Didn't know that was a part of this menu.

"All right, let's go see her," I said as I stood up.

When I exited the room, I found a line of people doing their best impression of a bucket brigade with sacks of something through the portal. I stopped briefly to look at them and then at my brother.

"This city's in bad shape, little sister. Many nobles have expectations and they want those met. Practically starved the common folk. All this is from back home, standard practice," he explained.

"That's generous," I said, a bit awed.

"Not really." Brother was an idiot sometimes, but he also had a good feel for things. "The expense with how our farms are now is really minimal; it's mostly just grain. For that, we buy the city's loyalty, because you'd better believe everyone is going to remember who starved them and who fed them when they needed it. Sure, it's the right thing to do, but it's also the right thing to do."

I thought about that for a few moments, ruminating on the past.

"Yeah, I suppose if someone had come to Orsken, driven out the soldiers, and fed everyone, lots of people would have loved them forever," I observed.

"It's why they loved you, Alana." I turned to look at him and he continued, "Maybe Mom kept you from hearing or seeing most of it, but you were loved. How many mother's children didn't starve because you gave them food? How many sons and daughters had something, anything in their bellies because you worked every day for it?"

I could see a few of the guards I'd brought along looking at me. In particular was a certain elf. He knew that my childhood home wasn't around anymore, and that I didn't really like talking about it, but I'd never gone into all the details with him. I didn't really like thinking about that time in my life, so he hadn't pried too much.

"We have things to do," I finally said. "Please lead us on."

Selene was in one of the nearby areas being used for the injured. She'd been assigned her own bedroom, and I was told she'd fallen asleep recently. I considered going in and waking her up, even against the suggestion of her caretaker, but passed. I could wait for a bit; it would probably give me better results if she were calm and clearheaded when we spoke. At any rate, I had most of what I needed, and plenty of work to do preparing the basic outline of my report. I could even draft it, so long as I didn't learn anything groundbreaking from her, then it wouldn't change much.

I made sure that someone would come and tell me when she woke and began the paperwork. I also began composing designs for testing these new gates. It was pretty easy to rule out some things with the models that we used, but without safety features there were things I wanted to test, no matter how much of a hazard it would be. All of my ideas got added to the list while I started to make up the basic safety guide we'd need for this. I was pretty sure Emperor Durin would want these done, if for no other reason than he might use the results as weapon ideas in the future.

A couple of hours into the work, I was joined by Father. He came down and pulled a chair opposite me, plopping down in it. He had a rather tired look to his features. At least he came bearing gifts, pushing me a bowl of the standard stew that ended up at any military base as soon as things started to settle. This was often served at Durin's fortress, and it wasn't bad, consisting mostly of vegetables and whatever meat could be found in a thick, goopy soup.

"You know, I shouldn't have to tell you to eat at your age, Alana," he commented, scooping some soup from his own bowl.

"Not like I've been here that long," I responded, setting my work aside and pulling the bowl close. I hadn't realized how hungry I was until the food was right in front of me.

"The sun went down a few hours ago, you do realize that, right?" He took a bite at the same time I did.

"I did not. How are things out there?"

"I've seen worse, but not in a while," he said, and I could feel the exhaustion in his tone. "I hear you had that gate destroyed, care to explain?"

"No, but it was necessary, trust me on that," I responded.

"Maybe, but several of my subordinates are in a bit of a fit over it. Claiming you had no right, and I've only not had you held because of our relation." There were types like that everywhere, it seemed.

I pulled the paper Durin had given to me and handed it over to him without a word. Dad's eyes got bigger as he went down, and I could see my own reaction from when I'd received it mirrored in him. He blinked a few times and reread it, as this wasn't something one saw every day.

"That's some paper, dear," he finally said as he passed it back.

"Don't I know it. I don't suppose you got any documents about the gate from our enemies?" I asked, hopeful.

"No, sadly they seemed to have evacuated everyone and everything important well before we took the place. Think they were a bit jumpy because you'd not been brought back or taken out, and were halfway out before the attack started."

"They didn't take Selene though, why?" I asked.

"Nothing confirmed yet. If it all fell apart and she escaped, then they'd have burned both of their bases if they moved her. It's also not easy to make the wards they had on those cells; stuff like that is planned out well in advance. At least that's what my advisors tell me, and they know their stuff better than I do." He took another bite while I thought.

"They planned to kidnap us well in advance then," I observed.

"Or planned to take any prisoners they could, we're unsure on that. Those cells were started at least a month before though."

We ate in silence for a while before another individual joined us, one of the medics. He was a bard, as were most of the medics for the army, at least on missions like this. They wanted priests to join, something that would have been really helpful for these field hospitals, but the orders had just been told about the gates not too long ago, so that didn't seem to be organized yet.

"The young lady just woke up," he informed us.

"How is she?" I asked.

"Physically? Bit malnourished, but nothing too bad. Mentally though, fragile, I'd say. Can't say I have a lot of experience with people being tortured, miss, but it looks like the kind of shock you see in soldiers after battles sometimes."

This world didn't yet have terms for things like post-traumatic stress disorder, but that didn't mean that it didn't exist. There were plenty of ways to be in situations that would leave you very messed up, and magical beasts or spellcasters in battles could do that kind of thing easily. There was some discussion if it was magically induced, or just stress, as one normally only found explosions and unstoppable monsters when magic was involved, but it didn't matter to most people either way.

"Let's keep the meeting to Ulanion and I. She knows both of us, so it shouldn't be too bad," I told everyone before we set out to her room.

CHAPTER 27

✦

THE BROKEN GIRL

"Come in," a small voice said after I knocked on the door.

I opened it and found myself in a small bedroom. It was nice, but simple, the bed and small desk taking up most of it. Selene looked to have just finished eating and stood as she saw us enter, rushing over and grabbing me in a tight hug.

"You're here," she said, almost sobbing. "They told me you left me, that you didn't care about me."

Carefully I wrapped her up, returning the embrace. "I didn't know they had you until I got back to civilization. Soon as we knew, they sent the army to come and save you. If I'd known . . ."

I didn't know what I would have done. It would be nice to say that I would have saved her, but truth be told I'd barely made it out myself. She needed someone to reassure her though, to let her share everything she'd felt. Nobody could really understand, could truly know how she felt, but we could be there for her while she tried to recover.

"Wait, how are you here?" she asked. "They just let you run back?"

"No, when the emperor heard about the portal, he sent a team out to investigate as quickly as he could. I came along to try and find out what was going on."

She looked a little off-put that I hadn't come for her, but for the item she'd made, but then something else seemed to click. "Then I can go home?"

"Of course, the portal's up and we can get you back when you're ready."

At that statement, she started crying in earnest. I sat with her on the bed while she let it all out. It felt like patience was going to be key here, and I needed to let her find somewhere she could feel safe. I had no idea if that was the right or wrong decision, but it was the best I had for the moment.

"I-I'd like to go now," she said when the tears finally stopped. It had been several minutes, and we'd ended up sitting on her bed while she let herself go.

"All right, do you have anything here you need to pack up?" When she shook her head, I continued, "Think you can answer a couple of questions for me while we walk?"

I wasn't qualified for this, but I did need information. As we stood and headed toward the portal, I made a brief stop to gather up my papers before we could continue. Unfortunately, some of the many guards that had been sent with me joined us as soon as we made it to the portal.

"Who are they?" Selene asked when she saw them, her grip on my arm tightening.

"Guards, to make sure we get back safe," I responded, signaling them to back off.

"Right, right, you said you had questions?"

"Yes, just confirmation. You said you made them three sets of gates?" I asked.

She nodded. "Yes."

"And this was the sequence you used?" I passed over a sheet with the written code.

"Yeah, they wanted it fast. I didn't want to, Alana, but, but . . ." She started shaking once again, and I could see the tears in her eyes. "He was a monster, a real monster. I had to, I had to . . ."

Before she could break down completely, I spoke, "It's okay, you're safe, nobody here is going to hurt you. The man, do you know his name?"

She shook her head. "He looked like a snake, like a viper in human skin."

That description rang all kinds of bells. I'd met one of the enforcers for the old royal family, and I could soundly believe that man had survived and was more than capable of torture. The memory of meeting him after escaping the underground sent shivers up my spine.

"Did he . . . ?" she asked, looking at me.

"I think I know who you're talking about," I said.

"He said things, about how you'd abandoned me, about how they'd get you back even though you ran away, about all the things he'd do to get you to talk . . . as he was doing them to me," she barely whispered the last part.

Behind her I could see Ulanion, his knuckles white as he death-gripped his sword, and the look of fury on his face alone would have sent more than one person fleeing. I gave him a quick glare. If Selene saw that it would be terrible, and he quickly schooled his face, nodding.

"No one is going to hurt you, Selene, you're safe. Those gates you made them may well kill the bastard too." That got me a weak chuckle from her.

"I hope so," she said. She knew as well as I how dangerous gates like that could be.

"Are you ready?" She looked up and realized that as we'd talked and walked, we'd finally made it to our destination.

It took me less than an hour after hearing what she'd said to prepare my formal report. I got the feeling the message that I'd sent to Emperor Durin had basically been turned right around to tell me to report to him with haste. The meeting room I was summoned to was quickly filling with a few of the individuals that were both stationed here and had relevant information.

Everyone stood as he entered, he quickly motioned for us to sit. The emperor was in a lighter armor, still his standard black, and looked like he'd been stressed the whole time I was gone.

"Sit, good news I hope?" he said as he took his place, looking at me.

"Sort of, we know they have two more sets of gates, the details on them were in the report. I'm worried that they're mental though, the men who are using them. The lack of any safeguard is bad for both us and them."

"Could you explain?" one of the administrators asked.

"Happily. If you placed one of the gates we use underwater, the water wouldn't pass through. I don't know if that is in the original design or not, but we put it there. There are also shutoffs, and protections if something is moving through. The gates aren't instant. Even though it may feel like that, there is a delay; ours have a small mana supply to keep them going for a few seconds to let things out, theirs don't. There's also the fact that if you put your arm in one of our gates and turned it off, the gate is pro-grammed to try to get you out of it—it's made to, but with theirs . . . hon-estly, I don't know what would happen." I could go on for days about this, protections for these were most of what I did.

"Those aren't built into the sequences already?" Emperor Durin asked.

"I have no idea if they are or not, since how the sequence works is a bit . . . unknown, just that it does. Would you, now knowing that, be will-ing to exclude them though? There are a lot on Ristolian's gates that are similar to ours, at least we think so, so either he was as paranoid as we are, or they aren't."

"Nobody tested that?" an outraged administrator asked.

"We've been trying to get a safe transport network up. That project has been very rushed, but since we were the only ones making them, there was no need to test dangerous models for safety. Now I would like to." I looked at the emperor, since we'd need his permission for that.

"I will of course consider that part of this investigation, and I believe I've already given you permission to do whatever you need." He gave me a pointed look. "For now, can they make more?"

"All indications point to no. That is the best piece of news." That got me a couple of nods, but the man who'd been questioning me had other thoughts.

"I hear that you destroyed the captured gate, would you care to explain yourself?" he asked, as if I'd done something wrong.

"Not really, since it should be clear from the explanation I've already given, but if you need it, fine. There was no way to keep it turned off, no way to stop them from returning through it, no way to do anything if they put a large mana supply on it and dropped it in the ocean. It was a safety hazard to not only the men I'd taken with me to investigate, but everyone in that city. I suspect they'd destroyed the other side anyway, but would you be willing to keep such a thing around?" The man flinched back at the acid in my voice.

"Her decision was the correct one. Both of you should calm yourselves though. It's clear we're all stressed and forgetting where our enemies lie." At the emperor's words, both of us bowed our heads.

"My apologies, the emperor placed his trust in you for this, and I shouldn't have questioned your judgment," the pencil pusher said.

"And mine. This day has been . . . trying, and I lost my temper." I still wanted to punch the man, but we needed to all work together, and cursing him out wouldn't help in either the short or long run.

Soon everyone was dismissed, and only myself and the emperor were left. He seemed to understand that I wanted to speak with him.

"Something else?" he said.

"Something personal. Selene is . . . not extremely close, but a friend. Will you see to it that she's taken care of?" I asked.

"I don't abandon my people when they get hurt, Alana; she'll get what help I can offer her. The orders will want to speak to her too, and they might well have someone better who can help. We'll let her decide what she wants, I think." He shook his head. "Torture . . . it's just not done. They're desperate, dangerous like a cornered beast. That is too far though. Even if they could gain support, the priests could turn on them for this, particularly because it was a girl they kidnapped from right outside Linden, madness."

"You think they'll care that much?" I asked a bit doubtfully.

"Alana, they've kept their rules in place by destroying those who disobey for millennia. Why do you think I am so generous toward them? Sure, it's the right thing to do, but history tells us clearly what happens to those who piss off priests too much, and it does so vividly."

"Good to know. Thank you for that," I said.

He patted me on the shoulder. "Of course, now go find a place you like and get to testing. We need to know how bad this could be."

"Gladly."

Glad you're back," Dras said as we met for lunch.

"Yeah, me too."

"Selene?" He looked up from his food questioningly.

"She's . . . rough, still refusing to travel much, and terrified. For now, she's taken up a position at the fortress, probably not the best thing, but we'll have to wait and see if she can be brought out of it." I had mixed opinions on how she was acting.

"You don't approve of it?" he asked.

"If she lets the fear take her, she may never recover. That said, I can't really blame her for being afraid. Crap, I'm afraid sometimes, and I didn't get anything nearly as bad as she did."

Two weeks after her rescue and there was still no sign of our enemies anywhere. I was nervous, and keeping guards nearby, but I still had things that needed doing, and locking myself up until the people who took us were caught just wasn't an option. That said, I was avoiding my family home, Mystien's lab, and anything even resembling a schedule when not firmly within friendly territory. Even my current project was being done under a false name.

"Not what I expected, but I guess you're probably right. Any chance you'll be coming back soon?" he prodded.

"Weeks at least, Dras, got something else I'm working on, and no, I can't tell you about it," I said, shaking my head.

"Wasn't going to ask. Shame though, we really need the help. After Linden, we got three more gate pairs set up and there are calls for dozens more. Emperor wants one in all the major cities for public use, and the military wants a bunch too. Their new eastern campaign looks like it's going to take a bit."

"Can't say the rush will be better for me, but at least I won't have managers and the like breathing down my neck the whole time." I laughed at his troubles; not that having a monarch wanting results as soon as physically possible was much better, but at least he was busy elsewhere.

He laughed right back. "I'm the one doing most of the breathing down necks nowadays."

"Careful there, Dras, or you'll end up in an office position forever."

"Would that really be so bad?" he asked, grinning.

"I think I'd go insane, personally . . ." Regardless of how much I complained about being sent all over the place, the idea of sitting in a workshop like that forever sent a shiver down my spine.

I thought back on things. I'd seen terrors, and horrors, and things that were well outside my ability to deal with. I'd been sent or drugged across continents and kingdoms. It had never been boring though, even when I'd been working in the labs, that had quickly turned into preparation for the expedition, and I could go enjoy the nightlife.

The project I was on now, though, was something else. I was the one in charge, and I could go where I wanted and do mostly what I wanted so long as I got results. I'd picked the place, and the team, and everything else about it, and that was fun too. It was research, but not the boring lab stuff, and I felt like I might really enjoy it this time.

We shared a few more jabs before lunch ended. Neither of us had much time; he had to get back to work, and I was only back in Lithere for the afternoon. On my way out, I was met by my bodyguard, who joined me in the carriage as we drove off.

"Anything?" I asked Ulanion.

"Not that I saw. We don't know he has people in Lithere, but if he didn't, I'd be amazed. Of course, nobody knew we were coming except Mystien, and if he's betrayed this empire we should consider returning to Atal."

I snorted at that one. "Luckily, I feel that to be quite unlikely."

I looked over at the many activation controls for the defenses on this carriage, just beside my seat. "I don't like playing bait, but if they are watching Dras, they're not going to let me just get away. Here, or when we leave the city, they'll strike."

The whole way back to the fortress, I was on edge, afraid that we were being watched, but as we made it to the area around it, some of that began to fall away. The empire was still enraged about all that had happened and really wanted a fight, but it looked like today we wouldn't be getting it.

On the other hand, there was much to do before I got to my next assignment. A messy process that I hadn't really done in either of my lives. Time seemed to slow as a maid helped me through it, her hands going through practiced movements. By the end I was thoroughly exhausted, but it was necessary for this task.

When I met Ulanion back at the gate, he just stared.

"How do I look?" I asked.

It was plain to see that he was trying to find a way not to step in the trap I just set for him. "It's . . . certainly different," he finally responded.

The black hair that spilled over my shoulders was indeed that. "Don't worry, I don't much like it either, and it's easy enough to be rid of. At least it should help with keeping me unrecognized, so long as someone keeps their helmet on." I looked at him pointedly.

"How exactly did I get assigned to this again?" he asked, putting on the conical helm that matched his armor. He looked like any other soldier in the empire's armies, not a knight, but one of the more common types.

"I trust you, and I need a guard. You've already seen enough of this stuff that there's no worry about having to bring you into secrets, and the less people who know the better, so you're the perfect choice," I said, defending my decision.

"Those are all good reasons, but what's the real one."

"I don't want to be lonely, and most of my former team is either buried under work or unable to join," I said.

"Fine then, I've had worse assignments." Grumble as he might, I could see the hint of a smile.

"You remember the cover story?" I asked.

"Why of course, Miss Jenna. We're only going to check on the area's food production and do some basic checks for issues, how could I possibly forget?" He dripped sarcasm, and I couldn't really blame him. The story was bland as plain rice, but it would do for our needs.

"Thank you, Sean, glad to see we're on the same page."

We chatted as we made our way to the gate. We left while the kitchens were serving dinner and almost everyone was gone, and that was by design. Our mission here would depend on security through obscurity, and the less people who knew anything, the better. I'd filed all the paperwork myself, and other than Father and the emperor, almost nobody knew where we were going. Everyone else involved in the whole thing was picked for a reason—that they didn't know us.

Both Ulanion and myself pushed down our auras hard as we came near, passing my brother, who'd been stationed here for tonight. He was the senior officer on guard duty, while everyone else was a brand-new transfer. I nodded and got a light wave before heading to the soldier directing people. He looked nervous and gave a rather worried smile as we came over to him.

"Ah, good morning, miss . . . do you have your paperwork?" I held out the little file, and he quickly read over it. "I see, I see, Gate 28 to . . . Silversprings? Never heard of that place . . . Um . . . right this way."

He led us over to the portal and ran through the standard start-up procedure. I really wanted to tell him how to do it the whole time because he was slow as maple syrup in winter, but we eventually got there. We waved as we passed through the gate to the way station on the other side.

The woman who greeted us on the other side looked a bit grumpy. Not too long ago these gates were used only for military purposes, but now they were being used for some minor pissant officials? Waste of the network, at least that was how a lot of people saw it.

Regardless, the small bags that we needed made it through, and there would be horses ready for us in the morning. While I would have loved to use a carriage, as my practice with sidesaddle was almost nonexistent, that would have been too expensive for who we were pretending to be.

"That's a big city," Ulanion observed as we set out. While it was still a couple of hours away, the ground here was flat, with the way station being on the only hill around; I suspected that hill was also man-made.

"It *was* a big city, now it's less than a thousand people. At least if tax records are to be believed." He raised an eyebrow, and not without reason. The place we were going was easy to pick out from the brownish grass all around it. "A couple hundred years ago, Silversprings was a big city—I'll let you guess their main export."

"Silver?"

"Right you are. You can't see it from here, but there are several small spring-fed lakes around the city, and it used to be one of the best mining towns around. Then the silver dried up. The farmland is, as you can see, poor, and while there's a bit near the lakes, beyond those and the fish there's not much here. Most of the people left, seeking better land elsewhere," I explained.

It was the perfect place for our testing. Banditry was not an issue, as there wasn't enough money or population for bandits to make a living. There was water for the tests we needed to use it for—a low number of people so hiding those tests would be easy—and if something did go horribly, horribly wrong, nothing of great value would be damaged.

The ride to the city was pleasant enough. This was close to the southern border of the empire, and it was noticeably warmer than what I'd been dealing with, but still mild. It was also just . . . calm, the whole place was just calm. There was the issue of the blisters I was developing, but while those were quite unpleasant, they would be easily healed once we finished our ride.

The walls grew and grew, and so did the signs of decay. While it looked impressive from far-off, you could see that they were barely being maintained. There was just too much area for the number of people they had, and large city walls like these were no small chore to keep clean. Someone was trying, that much was clear, but they needed help if they were to actually keep them in proper order. There were a couple of gate guards, who greeted us as we approached.

"Hail, travelers, don't suppose you're one Miss Jenna then?" one of the guards asked, looking over our clothes. I was dressed in what had become a sort of standard-issue black dress, often used by the female administrators of the empire, while Ulanion's armor matched well to the armor the two guards here wore.

"Indeed I am, not many travelers then?" I asked.

"Afraid not, ma'am, you're the first stranger we've had in a good bit, and the mayor's more than a bit nervous about your coming."

"Is that so?" I asked. "Are there any issues the city needs aid with?" I had a bad feeling.

"Well . . . maybe it's best if you speak to him," the man replied, looking a bit concerned.

Beside me, Ulanion sighed.

CHAPTER 29

✦

THE MANY WASTES OF
SILVERSPRINGS

Before we even made it through the gate, Ulanion was giving me a look along the lines of "can't you go anywhere there aren't problems?" It wasn't like I was looking for them, I was just really, abysmally unlucky. I didn't know what could be going on, but we'd have to see.

Once the gates were open, I was at least pleasantly surprised by what I found there. Most cities were crowded disasters with shouting and dirty streets. Normally there'd be a mass of folk near the gate, with inns and stables catering toward travelers.

Not here in Silversprings though. The gate opened into something vastly different. Near the gate was a small gatehouse and paddock for horses, but beyond that stretched something like a garden or field. You could see all the way to the noble's district, where another wall stood. From our point atop the horses, we could also see all around where poorer parts of the city would normally be, and most of those were nonexistent.

A guard mounted one of the horses here and began to lead us in.

"This is . . . certainly an interesting arrangement," I said as I looked around.

"Yeah, visitors always say that. Do you know the history of our fair city?" the man asked.

"Generally."

"Well, after the mines failed, people started to leave. Rich folks mostly at first, but then more and more regular people. Villages that had been outside the walls started to fail as there wasn't anyone to sell produce to, not that it was ever good farming here. We also ended up with the city becoming a ghost town, and for a while it looked like we might just . . . fade away," he said, looking at his home.

"What happened?" Ulanion inquired.

"Well, after most of the nobles left, one of their administrators got permission to do as he wanted. He began getting people into the upper city districts, while the old homes and businesses were broken down for materials and farmland. Figured that if we couldn't get much from outside, we could cannibalize the unused stuff, and wood has always been hard to get in this area."

"Reclaiming all the stone to repair walls, all the wood for . . . well lots of things. You'd even get the nails and the like back. Lots of hard work, but I can see it keeping your city afloat for a while," I observed.

"Yup, and stabilized it enough. Not having to move things so far helped a lot. A few people still get dregs of silver where they can for taxes, and the rest of us farm or maintain the city. It's not a bad life." The guard seemed happy with his home.

I continued to look at the farms. They were all far more compact than they'd be in a normal village, but you could see where the grazing animals were taken out the gate in the mornings, and how with their limited people they were working hard.

"I thought the mines had failed though?" Ulanion asked.

"Places like that never really run completely out of ore, just enough that it's not viable to run a large business from it. There's enough that the kids can help the old folks sort for anything useful, and a few men working can still pull some of the stuff up. We've got all the carts and tools, enough that if they're taken care of, they barely need any new ones. They were smart enough to pack up a lot of things in oil when the mines started to fail, hoping a new vein would be found, and so we open a new barrel of tools every now and then to replace what we've been using."

I was a bit amazed, it sounded like there'd actually been competent people running the place for the last couple of centuries, at least at the beginning. That wasn't what concerned me though.

"So, mind telling me what the problem is that the mayor is worried about?" I asked. I tried to plaster on my kindest smile, but I really wanted to know what was waiting for me.

"I'm not truly sure," he said, and at my raised eyebrow continued, "The man's just been running around like mad since we received word you'd be coming, trying to make sure everything was perfect."

That was unhelpful. It hardly mattered, though, as our ride had brought us to the upper district. The second gate was currently open, and it looked like this was normally the case. The delineation that normally existed between where nobles and commoners lived was this line, and while not all cities had an actual wall for it, this one did.

It was wild, truly wild, to see what had become of the mansions. Homes that would have belonged to either very wealthy merchants or lower nobility a few centuries ago were now estates for extended families. There were small gardens blooming on the large lawns, and children in simple clothes playing on the streets that would have been held under the tightest of security.

There were, of course, some things that didn't match; while the buildings were well-maintained, they were not being done up in the same way. There was nobody to pay for the expensive art, so what remained of the old pieces was not replaced. Instead the areas were covered with simpler things or very basic pieces. The glass windows were mostly replaced with wooden shutters, and I was sure that the insides of the houses had changed radically too.

These buildings and places were designed to last though. A noble estate would normally go through periodic upgrades here and there, but the structure itself was built and reinforced such that the family home would not fail for many, many generations. It was some sort of pride that your home had been somewhere for untold time, watching over your *lessers* or some such nonsense.

It looked like the extended families lived more communally here than in most places, but with the size of the buildings that wasn't odd, and with the size of the area, we soon found ourselves outside of a much more nicely made manse. It even had a separate wall around it and was much more well-maintained.

"The mayor's home? How's he affording all of this?" I asked. Doing that wouldn't be cheap.

The guard looked concerned at my question. "Oh . . . the mayor used to be a servant for the ruling noble, before Emperor Durin took over of course, and this house was kept for when the lord visited."

I raised an eyebrow. "How often did that happen?"

"Well, um, not in some time . . ."

There were a few people already waiting for us as we approached; someone must have seen us coming and sent word. I counted two maids, dressed in older, but still fairly normal outfits for the position, and one man who looked to be the butler. Why there were this many servants for the house of a mayor in a town this size, I didn't know, but I suspected there might be something odd going on.

The butler moved to help me down but was soundly beaten to the punch by Ulanion, who sent him a light glare, warning him off.

"Be nice," I said. The desire to help me down was welcome, but there was no reason for him to go and scare the poor people here.

"Welcome," the butler said as he bowed. "To Lady Jenna and her guard."

"You can drop the 'lady' part and just call me Miss Jenna," I said.

"Of course, my apologies. We've prepared rooms for your stay, of course, and reports on the city's state," he explained.

"Thank you, first I should speak to the mayor though. Could you please take me to him?" Whatever was going on, it would be best to get to the bottom of it first.

"Ah, that would be me, miss," the man said.

I was a bit taken aback at that, particularly with the uniform and all. I looked beyond him to the maids and squinted a bit. These two were definitely related, mother and daughter maybe? Definitely not too far-off, though it could be hard to tell with some small towns like this being very interrelated; the younger one also had eyes that would match the mayor, if I were any judge.

"I see, why are you dressed as a butler?" Sometimes it was just better to ask.

"Well, Miss Jenna, our family has served the ruling noble family of this region for years, and now that the emperor has seen fit to send you to take over, we'll be happy to serve you as well," he explained.

Things started to click into place.

"I'm not here to take over. There are no more nobles as such, you realize that, right?" Someone had done a piss-poor job of bringing this town into the empire, and some things would need to be explained. It wouldn't take too long to get things going right, I hoped, but it needed to be done. "I'm mostly here to look over the books and make sure that everything is in order, little more."

"I see . . . so you're not here to rule over us then?" he asked.

"No, you seem to be doing an acceptable job of that. None of the children I saw seemed to be starving and the infrastructure is in good order, those are the main concerns for now, but I need to know of any problems facing the area to see if we can't address them. Monsters, failing crops and the like. As I said, I'm also here to look over the books."

"Of course, I'll get them for you with haste. In the meantime, would you like to move to the offices then?" he asked.

"Let's," I replied.

The younger maid was sent off to prepare refreshments while we made our way into the mansion. Most of the things here were out of date by a decade or two, but if there was any wealth in the town, it was most definitely concentrated in this home. Everything was clean but didn't feel lived-in, like the covers were just taken off every now and then to maintain it, but nobody really cared about the place. It was still stuffed with art and the like though.

There was an office, presumably belonging to the former master of this estate, and a large enough table therein. The mayor grabbed one of the larger tomes and brought it over, standing to the side as I opened it up and found a seat.

"Please, join me," I said when he didn't sit.

The poor man was so used to being a servant that he looked quite uncomfortable. That needed to change, and as the tea was brought in, it began to. I ran through the town taxes, expenses, and incomes with him, and what I found was quite bothersome. More than half of the town budget was being directed to keeping this mansion in shape. There were even lists of all the expensive goods that were being bought periodically just in case someone important showed up. The tea, the wine, the bleeding fancy salts and sugars that were being bled in and basically given away to the people when they started to go bad.

I even took a few minutes to check, and it wasn't just random embezzlement. The mayor, whose name I learned was Mallowsweet, had kept meticulous records, and the goods were all dated, both from their acquisition and the date they were to be thrown out. He claimed the disposed goods were distributed evenly throughout the populace, which I believed but would be checking. It wasn't like there was a significant amount, just small quantities that made good gifts to the families in town about once a year.

By the end of it, I was tired. "Sir, your taxes are . . ." I had to check my notes. "At least thirty percent higher than the standard for the empire, and the wasted money on maintaining this house has to stop. We'll have to do some math, but there are no more nobles, and the . . ." I just sighed.

The poor man looked like he'd gone through half of the different forms of fear and despair throughout the day, and now was almost broken. "This is . . . I was so worried you'd be furious at what we were able to prepare in time for your coming, and . . ." He chuckled once. "I'll be glad to save the money, but the children will be so disappointed; during the harvest festival, we always used the old sugar to make them sweets."

"Get beehives and use honey instead. As for the other indulgences, the citizens will have to do with new, but slightly lower quality goods. Which won't be a problem for them to afford when we're done, good grief." I shook my head.

"Beehives?" he asked.

"I'll make note that you need a few craftsmen for some of the newer technologies in the empire, but yes, you can farm bees, and with your local gardens and I'm assuming wildflowers in the spring, it should be easy. Maybe even a good new source of income for you." The idea of replacing silver with liquid gold nearly made me laugh.

I soon had dinner, which was a ludicrous feast, but I ate and even asked the mayor and his family to join me. The room they'd prepared was almost like my parents' room back home, if not nicer, and while it was dumb, I'd take it for now. I needed to get to testing tomorrow, now that the act had been fulfilled, though in the evenings I'd take some time to sort the town out and make notes on the specialists they needed, both for the act and because it would actually help these people.

✦

POKING AROUND

The next morning, I met up with Ulanion; he'd been put in the room beside my own since he was a guard, but he joined me for a very quick breakfast. After that, I began to move out into the town, taking with me some of my supplies, and notably the gates I needed to test. My hope was to do a quick walk around town to keep up appearances, and then head to the lakes for some testing. Today would be the lightest workload if we got to it, and would also serve as a scouting day for locations.

The mayor met us as we made our way to the front door of the house. Someone must have given him a heads-up on our movements, since he was chipper as he stood by the door. I wasn't sure that I loved the implications of that; if we were followed later in the day, it might really cause problems. I'd have to warn someone off if we saw them, and if they persisted, it would be bad. Our true mission was, after all, still quite secret.

"Good morning, Miss Jenna, Mister Sean, did you have something you needed? I'd be quite happy to help." The man did look that, bouncing on his feet as he spoke.

I was glad to see he'd dropped the "lady" part, and though his dress was still that of a servant, it was no longer the butler uniform, wholly unsuited to so many forms of work. "Unfortunately, I must decline. We need a good idea of the area and what is going on, and I'd be worried people would feel intimidated by having the mayor there with us."

"Ah . . . I mean no disrespect, but I'm afraid that as strangers and with an armed guard, they may feel intimidated regardless," he said, truly looking nervous. It saddened me to see we hadn't quite got past that little worry.

"Perhaps, but I shall not change my decision on this," I said with finality.

The man visibly paled, as if he'd stepped on a landmine. I could see the gears ticking, thinking that he might have offended me and what I might do. I couldn't let him do what he wanted, but I also needed to keep from looking too scary.

"Forgive me . . ."

"There is nothing to forgive, Mayor Mallowsweet, simply that I must do things properly, and I cannot have you following me as I do so." As I spoke, I smiled slightly, trying to put him at ease.

"Of course, if you do need anything at all, please let me know." He quickly moved from the way, letting us pass without another word.

"He was afraid," Ulanion said once we were well outside of hearing range.

"He's used to serving nobles. It used to be really bad, particularly for non-magic users. He doesn't know us, who we are, or how much power we could bring to bear. For all he knows, I could order you to cut off his head and nobody would care," I explained.

"You could, and they probably wouldn't."

"Perhaps," I agreed. "But I wouldn't, and at any rate, I doubt the emperor would look kindly on me killing the man without a good reason. He might not do anything about it immediately, but such an act would stain my reputation for good, and that of the empire as a whole. I think I'd soon find all future opportunities in any position with even a bit of power drying up should word get back to him about something like that."

I could see him frowning. "You make it sound like a logical choice; shouldn't it be a moral one?"

"Both work out the same," I said. "While I wouldn't want to hurt him because it would be wrong, it would also be the wrong thing to do even if it weren't. That's one of the things I do like about the new regime, they try to make doing the right thing the easiest; it gets rid of the temptation."

"Are you tempted by power?" he asked.

"Everyone is, even if they want to do the right thing. *Especially* if you want to do the right thing. If someone is in your way, it's just so easy to justify crushing them, to make yourself think they deserve it. Sometimes they do, sometimes they don't, but the longer you go down that path, the easier it is to always convince yourself they do."

"You sound like him," Ulanion said, very quietly.

"He learned a hard lesson; one I don't aim to repeat. I don't know what happened, but I think he was right, and I think he meant what he said. I also lived in a little village like this, and I know what it's like to have someone abuse your people because they can. Though if I'm honest, I never got it as bad as a lot of people did," I answered.

"It was that bad here in the human lands then? I knew it was bad, but most people don't like to talk of it."

"It was like the village we all saved. Except that rather than some magical beast stalking us, it was starvation. It was everywhere, slowly withering people away, and it was horrible. There wasn't any escape," I whispered.

"That's something I admire about you." At my raised eyebrow, he continued. "You don't give up, and I've never seen you be cruel, even when many people would be. If it's right or easy, it doesn't matter. How many people do you think have seen the things you have? I've spoken to your brother, you know, and to Dras. They've told me some of the stories of your adventures."

"Did they now? Ah, at any rate." I finished speaking and pointed to the little shop we were approaching.

The rest of the day was spent going around the town and asking questions about the goings-on. Over and over we got similar answers, that everything was in excellent order and that everyone was happy. I didn't really expect any open dissent after speaking to the mayor, and half suspected that he'd told everyone to be on their best long before I got here.

That said, it wasn't useless, and I did learn a good few things. The town had issues getting lumber. Importing it wasn't really viable, and there weren't any trees normally growing around here. There was one older bard woman who lived in the town who kept a small patch, but she had to put those out sparingly, as even with her powers, growing them was difficult.

Said bard and her son were the only magic users in the town. The young man was spoken of quite highly by several of the girls I met, and I had to remember the reputation most casters of my type garnered. More private conversations, where I pulled some people to the side away from Ulanion, confirmed that there weren't any major abuses in the town other than a few guards that sometimes got a little too proud of their authority here. Most were quite pleased with the empire though.

I made a few notes. Someone might read these reports, as half-done as they were, and if they did, this little town might get a few people to help. A note was also sent to the bard and her son, asking for a meeting sometime in the next few days. They could in fact tell me no; as casters they had that privilege, but I doubted they would.

By noon, we were done in the town and moved to the nearby country-side. I dreaded having to ride again, but it would be too much to just walk around, so get our horses we did. The information I had indicated some potential spots I could use for my experiments, but like with so many things, there was no way to know for sure their suitability until I got there and saw them for myself.

We rode out of the town and out into the savanna opposite of our entry, toward the lakes. It wasn't a far ride to get there, less than an hour if I had to guess, and it was interesting to see we weren't the only ones here. These little bodies of water weren't huge, but they were big enough, and this was also where the mines were located.

There were a few old people at one of the shores near a well-worn path to said tunnels that greeted us. They were using the water to clean the little bits of rock and ore, expertly looking through them for the bits of silver this town used for its taxes.

"Greetings, elders," I said as we approached. A few started to try and rise. "Please, don't stand on my account. Does all go well?"

"Aye, Lady, all goes quite well," their representative, a truly ancient man said.

"Please, call me Jenna. The title ill suits me since I'm no noble, just someone sent to make sure the town is well after the regime change."

"I see, the mayor went on and on. So that means you're not staying?" he asked.

"No, though your town is lovely. Are there any issues you can think of that might need solving?" I replied.

"Hmm, there are problems, always are, miss. They aren't taking our boys to die in war anymore though, and the taxes have gone down since the emperor took over, long may he reign." The last part was accompanied by a bit of a salute, an old gesture some people used when talking about the previous king in public.

"Do you mean any issues, miss?" one of the women asked, and at my smile and nod, continued, "That boy caster, Sloan, is a menace. Chases any-thing with teats, including, I think, one of old Ralph's mares." There was a good round of chuckles at that one, and a few scandalized looks. "Several of my granddaughters will have trouble finding husbands if he puts babies in them, you know." She shook an old, crooked finger as she spoke.

I tried, and failed, not to laugh. "If he's not being forceful, there's not too much I can do, but I am planning on meeting him soon and we'll see if we can't tell him to calm it down a bit."

"Better than his mother's done," the old woman grumbled, before several of her peers finally shushed her.

Our talk done, we kept moving outward. Very quickly we found ourselves far from anything the town was doing. There was nothing wrong with the land near the city, so there was no reason to go this far away from it. With the population they had, these places were mostly abandoned anyway, just a few old, crumbling ruins from the days when the area was used.

We passed several small lakes until finally coming to a larger one.

"We need some depth; don't suppose you'd be willing to check it for me?" I asked.

He shook his head, and began removing his armor. It would be heavy and rust at any rate. By the time he got to the lower layer of clothing, he must have realized I was looking at him and met my eyes.

"Seriously? Did you plan all this out from the start?" he asked.

"No, just a happy accident," I replied with a smile.

Without hesitation he lost the shirt, and then his pants as well, crossing his arms and glaring as he stood there nude. I felt my face go beet red and covered my mouth. Keeping my eyes where they should be was not the easiest thing in the world as he spoke.

"It's rude to stare, you know, but if I remember correctly, you don't seem to mind nearly as much as your friends." With that he turned, giving me quite the view as he made his way into the lake before diving.

The horses looked at me like I'd lost my mind as I wheezed in laughter.

CHAPTER 31

✦

FLIRTING AND TESTING

I was still a bit pink-faced when Ulanion left the lake, strolling out like he was in a superhero movie.

"So . . . how deep is it?" I asked, covering my face.

He laughed before answering, "About twenty feet."

I could stand there flirting all day, and perhaps doing other things . . . but time and place. Neither were correct for this, and so, with an effort, I schooled myself.

With a small frown, I looked up at the sky. "Getting late in the afternoon already, and we'll need to set up some wards before we do anything major; might be better to come back in the morning so we can spend all day. Then again . . . perhaps I should have tried to get someone who could build us a structure, but that would have just brought in more people, and caused more problems." I began to pull out my tools as I mumbled to myself, "Got a couple of the safer tests we can run, but you'll be swimming a bit for it. Could you place this in shallow water?" I asked as I handed him one of the gates.

The gates for this mission were small, very small, and by design. I neither wanted something too large to control nor too cumbersome for me to easily carry. Most of the space for them was the added places for power supply. I began the most basic shield setup; it was the one I needed for this one particularly. The gate went a dozen feet in front of me with the exits pointing at a right angle. This should be safe, but procedure and all that.

When Ulanion had returned from his mission, I let him into my shield and pulled him over.

"All right, starting in 3, 2, 1" Then I used a small movement spell to switch on my gate.

"That's . . . underwhelming. Why couldn't we do this back in the city?" he asked.

Out of both sides of the gate was a light trickle, pushing water out to the sides lighter than even a weak pump.

"I don't remember all the math for water pressure, and wouldn't bore you with it if I did, but water is dangerous," I answered as I flipped off the device.

"I mean, that tracks I suppose, did you learn anything?"

"Yes, but I need you to go move the portal in the water down to the very bottom, if you don't mind."

When I repeated the test at a lower depth, I could only frown.

"Not good?" Ulanion asked.

"No, they don't stop water and the stream is larger, meaning the pressure matters."

"How bad?"

I made a face. "Bad, bad. What if I dropped one end in the ocean? You can see the difference between even a low and high depth, so we need to run a couple more tests while we're here."

I repeated the test several times, recharging, and even using a small magical stopwatch to time the whole affair. Notes were made in a small pad, and I found some things that were at least slightly promising.

For one, the gates cared about matter going through. With larger ones and the sheer mass of mana we were shoving into them, it didn't matter for personnel transport, but it would here. There was a distinct increase in mana cost between being open to air, being underwater, and being deeper underwater, displayed in the time it took the gate battery to drain itself.

Ulanion looked bored, and during the longer time testing the mana consumption rate, had even taken to putting his pants back on while I waited, the spoilsport. There wasn't all that much for him to do here, other than keep an eye out, and this place was deserted. Once or twice he went to go look at something, but it was just small birds or local wildlife.

We got back quite late, and I could tell that the mayor was stressed as soon as I entered the house.

"Oh, thank goodness, you're all right." He sighed.

"I'm quite fine, I do have a guard with me. Was there some worry that I might be hurt?" I asked.

"Well, nobody saw you for most of the day, and people started to get worried . . ."

"That is normal, and will continue. I will be spending much of my time over the next few days outside of the city, but I assure you Sean can keep me safe," I said mildly.

"I could ask a few of the guards to accompany you," he offered.

"Unfortunately, that is not acceptable. There are things I need to check on privately." Not a good answer for him, but an honest one, at least.

"Ah yes, of course, my apologies," he said as he bowed.

"Please don't be so formal. It's rather distracting." I sighed.

"I simply don't wish to disrespect you, ma'am. If our manners are improper . . ."

"Not at all. I actually come from a farming village not much different in size from this one. The emperor cares not about birth, but about ability, remember that."

He looked stunned, and a bit put off, as if he was unsure of how to treat me now. I'd made sure that my cover story was near enough to my own life, and I was certainly no noble. Even though I'd told him that many times, I felt he was now starting to get it. Of course, if he started being rude or snippy, I could still put him squarely in his place.

"But your math and understanding of finances are . . . the daughter of a mayor?" he inquired.

"I would prefer it if you didn't mention my family again, but no, simply schooled well. My hometown, like many others, fell during the war and I was given the opportunity to learn afterward." I could see him tense a bit, then relax once more.

"This is all still quite strange to me," Mallowsweet admitted.

"Indeed, it seems like whoever brought you in when the land was taken over was rather lax about informing you of policy. One of my notes is that you are in need of assistance on that matter and a few others. Still, the town is otherwise doing pretty well."

Over the next two days, I brought out some basic measurement tools and continued with the water testing. It wasn't much, but this was one of the easiest abuses I could think of, and the damage would be unbelievable. In that time, I managed to establish a rough baseline of mana consumption to water amount, but that was . . . very much an "about this much" statement. I could hand off the information for others to investigate in depth, and in greater depths if the conclusion was decided to be something to look into.

I kept meticulous notes in English, as I didn't want to even imagine the repercussions if these fell into the wrong hands. Sure, there were a few people who would understand, but unless that ancient priest was teaching classes, it wouldn't be many. Justin had seemed content to not spread it, and even the original portal maker had not spread the language far and wide, though he could have.

The mayor was giving me increasingly weird looks when I came back to town. His curiosity wasn't good, but there wasn't much I could do about it either, and sadly, the next morning I had a meeting.

The pair of bards showed up right on time, though with the general prevalence of timekeeping in this world they were simply supposed to show up between breakfast and lunch. Still, that was something, if they'd wanted to try and throw their weight around by making me wait, I would have just had to deal with it.

The first was an older woman in her fifties, perhaps early sixties, and well-dressed compared to the rest of the folks in town, with the obvious exception of the mayor. She had a light smile on her face and didn't seem much bothered by anything.

Behind her came a man who I could only compare in my head to Jackson. His clothes were, by a mile, the flashiest I'd seen here, brightly colored and hanging on him loosely. They were still of a village make, but on the far nicer scale. Appearance-wise he was tall, well enough built and equipped with the good looks that said he spent a lot of time on himself. I instantly disliked him.

"My apologies, my lady, as I haven't yet made your acquaintance. Had I but known that such a beautiful woman was the one requesting a meeting, I would have of course come far quicker. Though taking one's time isn't a bad thing either . . ." He smirked suggestively.

I returned it with a gentle smile of my own. "I'm here in an official capacity, Mister Sloane, so kindly drop the flirting."

He didn't look like he knew what to say to that one, but his mother laughed.

"Oh, I like you, my dear, dealt with a lot of skirt-chasers before?" she asked.

"Several, and one particularly brazen one comes to mind, though he was never much interested in me. Shall we begin?" I said, motioning to their seats.

CHAPTER 32

✦

PREPARING FOR THE SHOW

For the record, you are Mary and Sloan, yes?" I began.

"That's quite so," the woman answered for both of them.

"Excellent, you may call me Jenna. I'm here to look for issues with the administration of the town and rectify them, if possible."

"We're a fairly small town, miss, other than a few frankly minor gripes, there's not much," Mary said.

"There's a lack of wood, my understanding being that you two are the only producers in town. While there's enough here for the town to support itself for now, that will cause problems in the long run. Are there any other things like that?" I asked.

Sloan smiled, leaning in. "There were a few monsters a couple of years back, but nothing we couldn't handle." He puffed his chest out, but frankly I'd seen enough monsters that I wasn't that impressed. Though if there was a problem, it would need to be looked into.

"What kind? From where, when, and how many?" I asked.

"Engorged snakes, around a dozen or so two years back, though we've seen two or three smaller ones since. As for the where, the old mine. They'd nested down there and nobody realized for far too long. Between us and the guards, it wasn't too much of an issue, but they had the wicked ability to speed themselves up," Sloan said with a smile.

"He's right, probably from some old busted magical items leaking magic into the mines somewhere. We found a few near the main nest, but there might well be more down there," his mother added.

"Has nobody gone down and cleaned them out?" I asked.

"Sure they have, but there's hundreds of years' worth of tunnels down there, following veins in random ways and directions. It's a maze even to the people who know it well, and not really worth it to go off of the main tunnels if you want to find things. They had mages back in the day, at least a few, to shore things up and put spells where they needed to go, but records of what's where get lost." Mary couldn't do much more than shrug.

"Might need to send someone out to check those . . ."

"I'd recommend against it, dear. As the spells off the main branches fail and the supports get older, the unused tunnels get more and more dangerous. They collapse periodically, nothing much we can do about it." Mary was just a wealth of information, though nothing quite what I wanted to hear.

"Very well, I suppose I'll have to inquire with the mayor further about where they go and maps and whatnot."

"I can tell you that they at least extend away from the town," Sloan offered. "I could even take you down into some of them if you would like to . . ." He cut that attempt off, I suppose upon seeing the deep frown Ulanion was giving him.

"On a more productive note, can I convince the two of you to expand your tree-growing operation a bit?"

The mother looked at her son and shrugged. "Sure, might have to ask some of the town to gestalt with us sometimes if you want that though."

"And there's no other magically able person in town, no other members of your family?" I asked.

"I have only one child, and his father is dead," Mary said, continuing after seeing me flinch. "It was a long time ago. As for grandchildren . . ."

All eyes fell on her son, who looked uncomfortable. "I . . . don't know of any children I've fathered . . ." he began.

"I'll add a request for a visit from a priest of Lovers."

"Eh, I'm sure it'll work itself out," Mary said, smiling. Like many mothers, it seemed she wanted to add grand to her title, though her lack of care on how that happened bothered me.

There were only a couple more small issues to go over for the sake of paperwork. As soon as we were done, I went to go and find the mayor. I had questions about those tunnels.

"If there were any full maps, Miss Jenna, they were lost some time ago," he said. "Though I doubt they ever existed."

"Can you clarify?" I asked.

"Originally, the mines were a series of caves, big, but natural, and they were expanded. I know that the orders were specific that they always move away from the town, but beyond that, not much. I can dig you up the maps we do have, miss, but I will advise that they are very incomplete."

"Look them up when you can. I don't plan on going down there myself, but I'd like to call in someone to check it out. Particularly if there are monsters down there. Who knows, if they've got some valuable materials in them, you might end up making the town some money off of it all."

After that, I spent several days setting up to go back to testing. The next test was what would happen if something was inside the gate when it was turned off. I knew what the normal ones would do, since they'd had more than a few protections put in for just that happening.

First and foremost, none of our gates were supposed to shut down if there was anything in transit. If something was, it would be gently pushed out of the gate while it went through the shutdown process. Gently was relative, as the force would increase quite quickly if it remained inside more than a second, in order to clear it. We'd discussed trying it out a few times in the past, but with the amount of mana the main gates used normally, few things would ever be able to resist, so it was a bit of a moot point.

"All right, I'm about to drop it," I said to Ulanion as I prepared the off switch.

"Right then, whenever you're ready."

With the flipping of the switch, I got to see something truly new. The gates really did not like it, and there was a brief moment where a special stream connected the two, accompanied by a pained ripping sound. I even got to see the plane of the portal roil and leave its place inside the circle for just a few moments.

"Let's go see what we've got," I said excitedly as the process ended.

"Carefully," he advised.

As we walked up to the small pair of magical items, I could see the distortion in the air where they'd been.

"Now that brings back memories," I observed.

"Hmm?"

"When I was learning to make portals, I got that a lot. It's weird, but mostly harmless if it's the same. Hmm, for the sake of safety and repeatability we'll need to move a bit, and see what happens when they're further apart."

I probed the distorted area with a small stick, but it seemed that it was just as harmless as the ones I'd created, just very disturbing to look at.

"Please be careful, Alana."

"No worries, like I said, I've seen these before. I'm also not putting my hand or anything in it," I said as I waved off his worries.

"Will this persist?" he asked.

"For a while, have to note that down."

The gates had survived with no damage so far as I could tell. I knew a good bit about the construction of magical items, and these had no issues at all. A brief test also revealed that they still functioned fine. That was a relief, as replacing any of these would be a real pain—doable, but a pain.

The little metal rod we were using for our tests wasn't so lucky. It had been badly mangled, stretched, and pulled in unnatural ways before the portal spat it out. The ends that had been inside seemed to have undergone some kind of spaghettification before the portal snapped shut. There was no two ways about it, if an extremity had been in there the best you could hope for would be severe injury, but a head or vital organs and you'd surely die. That wasn't outside of expectation though, so I just shrugged.

Like all good scientists, I needed to repeat my test.

The results were much the same regardless of distance between the gates. There were a few differences, mainly in the leftover distortion. If they were further away from one another, the distortion between the two was smaller, and the bulk of it faded faster. There was still a small one near the gates themselves that was a bit more persistent, but not so much as when they were closer together. Soon enough, that line of questioning, too, had been exhausted.

I finally sighed in relief when we got to the last test. I was spending so much time away from Silversprings that it was beginning to raise questions. There were excuses in plenty, of course, and I had all the authority I needed to keep doing as I wished, even if they found out that I was lying, but it would be inconvenient.

There was only one question left. Could you make a pseudo-orbital bombardment? We'd be working with much smaller projectiles, of course, mostly a small, pointed bit of enchanted steel. My main fear was what would happen if we were close when it went off, and so for this test we were on the other side of the pond we'd been using, in a comfortable little trench Ulanion had dug for us.

The setup was simple enough. There was a pair of gates, one above the other and facing so that the steel ball could travel down. Plumbing them had been a pain, but very important for this, as were the enchantments on the steel ball, making sure that it wouldn't go off course. It also increased speed downward, this was needed as there was going to be air resistance regardless of what we did. In space, this would be far worse.

Below the first pair was another gate. This gate's sister would be pointing the soon-to-be-very-fast-moving object harmlessly into the lake. I expected an explosion of some size when it was fired and prepared my wards accordingly.

I floated the steel ball in place with a simple movement spell while we moved to the trench. Wards were turned on and prepped, and finally I set it to go. This was sure to be a show.

CHAPTER 33

MISTAKES WERE MADE

Things began, as they often do, so easily. At my mark, the portals flipped on and the projectile was released. This was all according to plan, all exactly as I suspected it should be. The little steel ball fell, and accelerated in its fall, toward the portal, only to reappear back above, continuing the cycle. It was draining mana from the portal, but for this particular test I'd made sure to fill the very significant mana storage on both portals to make sure it wouldn't fail before we got a good speed on the thing.

"Is this really dangerous?" Ulanion said, seemingly unconvinced after only a few seconds.

"Oh, you'll see, it most definitely is," I assured him, watching the projectile move faster and faster.

For the first few moments, it was rather normal, rather boring even. There was still air resistance, and even once it had broken past terminal velocity, it took a bit for it to get going well. As the moments turned to minutes though, things began to change.

"That's pretty quick, faster than most arrows, for sure," Ulanion observed. "And a steel ball like that will make quite the dent."

I just chuckled and let it run.

There was a whooshing noise that grew, and grew, and grew until.

CRACK!

"Just broke the sound barrier, like a whip when snapped," I said.

From there, nothing too interesting happened for a little bit. The portals had a nasty wind going between them and kicking up dust all around, and they were pretty noisy, but that was all within expectations. They were also drawing mana faster than I might have expected, but with their reserves and the fact that the missile wasn't that big, it was no major issue.

"Alana, something's happening. It's turning . . . reddish?" I couldn't see that much from here, but I trusted Ulanion.

"Yeah, it's heating up from all the rubbing against the air. The enchantment on it should help keep it from melting or anything though."

The noise grew, and the light coming off the little steel ball grew too, until it was straw yellow and bright, and making a sound like a jet taking off. I checked the mana level, as I'd planned to let it run until the first pair ran out, but with where things were, I wasn't sure that was a good idea. The horses were even further than we were, almost a mile away, and they were looking very scared from their tied-up positions, it almost looked like they were trying to pull the ties from the ground.

"That's enough, turn it off!" Ulanion shouted over the racket. The noise was getting worse by the second, but hadn't reached the level or sudden escalation that would trip the wards to block sound.

With a quick movement I slammed the off switch, sending the projectile into a safe section of ground. The wards did activate on that one, though I could still feel the ground shake and shudder as the little steel ball rocketed into the dirt, sending up a huge shockwave and cloud of dirt.

That was when things started to get weird. The gates the ball had been circling in, or at least where they were when the explosion went off, started to glow a brilliant blue. I couldn't see the gates themselves, as the cloud expanded, churning and distorting the air. It almost looked like a giant balloon was being blown up, but in a small space. Bigger and bigger the light got, until it hit something.

It hit one of the distortions from our previous experiments. I thought they'd closed, but apparently I was wrong—they'd just shrunk. As that blue light touched them, they too started to grow, grow and expand, and the light jumped from one to the other, all along the other side of the lake.

I knew they were expanding because I could hear the sucking of air, the water from the lake, and in places where the distortions came close to the ground, the ground being sucked in like a vacuum. It was much like the sound the weapon had made, only a thousand times more eerie. The various bits of matter floated, suspended in misshapen whirlwinds as the ripples in space expanded, even from our perspective, moving out from where they'd been before.

"Oh, shit," I said, watching as the expansion began to quickly slow.

Iron hands grabbed me and pulled me down into the trench, not a moment too soon. As I looked up and tried not to scream, I saw the wards activate to stop the incoming shock wave, and then shatter like glass. I closed my eyes and pulled into the man holding me against him as the blast washed over us with an ear-shattering *BOOM!*

I knew it only lasted seconds, but it felt like a lifetime as the explosion worked its way out and then came back in with a roar, pulling the matter lost back to where it belonged. The wind made my hair tangle all around me, and it felt like I struck a brick wall at a full run once in each direction, knocking the wind clear from my lungs.

When it finished, Ulanion helped me to sit up. I was shaking, my hands moving on their own like I was cold. He was saying something, again and again, but I couldn't make it out. The only thing I could hear was painfully loud ringing as the damage to that sense began to set in. He placed both hands on my shoulders and looked at me, lips moving again and again.

It took a second to process that he was saying my name, over and over. Another moment and my thoughts began to finally arrange themselves into something even resembling order, and I started to understand just how close I'd come to dying a moment ago. Curious, I put one hand up to my left ear, and it came back coated in red. That wasn't good, that wasn't good at all.

I put a finger to my boyfriend's lips to calm him and began to sing. It was hard as I couldn't hear myself at all, and he looked less than pleased, but I needed to be able to hear, and I was guessing he did too. Ears for both of us came first, and as the shock began to fade and my ability to perceive sound returned, I started to find a number of smaller injuries. I was covered in small bruises everywhere from being pushed so hard, and a more general healing spell took care of those.

When I finished, I was greeted with crystal clear sound, and one I really did need to hear.

"Alana, are you okay?"

"Shaken, but alive. That . . . was unexpected," I answered, pulling my finger away.

"What happened? That was not supposed to happen, right?" he asked.

"Not sure, either the explosion from the ball hitting ground and breaking something, or it not being all the way through one of the gates when they cut off, or some interaction between them and at that speed, or some combination of all of the above. Those little distortions weren't closed though, that's for sure, and it tore them right back open and filled them with . . . stuff. I think the explosion was them expelling that stuff, but again, I don't know for sure."

"Okay, I'm going to pop up and see what it looks like, give me a moment." He did just that, and I could see him stiffen. "Alana, I think you need to see this."

I rose. The trench we were in was falling apart, the dirt having shifted. Even as I braced a hand on it, dirt shuddered and poured into the hole, a large section of the wall just crumbling down. Once I saw it, I knew I must have looked much like he did.

The crater was easily three hundred feet across, and nearly half as deep. It looked like something out of a WWI movie, one of the places artillery had fallen and made a hole, only so very big. Floating in the center, and all around what used to be the far bank of the little pond were writhing blobs where light moved in odd ways, the distortions we'd seen blown up orders of magnitude in scale. Even the air around the crater itself looked . . . off, like the light was bending ever so slightly.

As for the pond, most of it was gone. What water there was left in the small lake was pouring in and disappearing into the bottom of the crater. There was something down there, far below the messed-up space and in the lake bed, but I couldn't see it. Whatever it was, the remnants of the water were being consumed, fast.

"We're going to need help with this." It sounded stupid but it was the only thing I could think to say.

"I'm going to get the horses. Are you good to stay here for a few moments?" Ulanion asked.

"Yeah, yeah, I'm good."

I sat there, watching, looking upon the destruction I'd so carelessly wrought. I'd been so excited about this, so happy to see what would happen after so many tests where nothing had gone awry. Now . . . it was possible to slowly fix some of the distortions I'd seen before when my portals were less clean, but they were nothing compared to what I could see now—just little blips. If I had time, and lots of help, perhaps I could do something, but alone . . . it was unlikely.

Oddly, the water just kept coming. All these little lakes must have been connected somehow by more than the surface creeks we'd seen, because this one was looking quite dry, yet still more arrived from somewhere. It sounded almost like someone had taken the stopper out of a bathtub, but a bit louder.

"I can't find them," Ulanion said about fifteen minutes later when he returned. "They're not that important, we need to go, we need to get . . . I don't even know."

"I'm sorry, I didn't . . ."

"Not your fault, nobody could've known this would happen."

"Still . . ."

"Come on, we need to get back to the way station, I'll carry you," he said as he gently helped me up.

I was thinking about how to climb on his back when he laughed, scooping me up. "Only one way to carry you . . . Your Highness."

I tried to punch him, but he was already running and fast, and I was held tight as he bolted across the plains. Had to admit though, it did lighten the mood just a bit.

CHAPTER 34

CONNECTION LOST

The hills blurred by us as Ulanion ran. We left the giant spacial distortion floating there, and the hole in the bedrock that was slowly draining the local water sources down into . . . wherever it went I wasn't honestly sure. As we moved, I got a close look at the landscape. Nothing was too obvious outside of the immediate blast zone, since there were no trees to knock down, nor stones to shatter. As we moved away from the scene of destruction, everything seemed to be normal. Some of the grass was perhaps pushed back a bit, but nothing too out of the ordinary.

The exception was the sky, which had a huge cloud over where we'd been. A massive amount of rock, dust, and water had been thrown in every direction, and that would be visible for miles with the flat lands here. It only became more and more clear where we'd been as we moved from the site.

"Are you good?" I asked to the running soldier, trying not to focus on the speeding ground below me.

"Fine, this isn't anything, just hold on." It didn't even sound like he was out of breath as he spoke, just like he was going for a light jog.

We circled wide around the city, which was just a white blob on the horizon. Getting spotted wouldn't be acceptable, and we didn't have time to waste. We needed help, and needed it now. I let the minutes pass as the winds pulled and tugged at my dress, making it flap wildly in the wind.

Soon enough we came upon the way station, the hill rising before us before Ulanion slowed. There was our ticket home, and to gather aid.

"Others are here," he said in a low voice, pointing to several horses tied up nearby.

He set me down and together we walked to the door. As fate would have it, none of the other guests were there, or happened to be peering out the window to look as we'd been approaching. Before I could reach forward, the door opened of its own accord, the person inside trying to leave.

"Who . . . oh, thank goodness, you're alive, the mayor is panicking!" The man in the doorway froze for a moment to process before speaking, letting a great breath out. I recognized him as one of the servants from the manor; apparently he'd been dispatched here. "He's currently forming a party to look for you, but . . ."

"We'd circled around the city and were near enough to make our way here instead of returning. The horses spooked and fled. Please tell the mayor that I'm fine. Are there reports of other injuries? Or what happened, exactly?" I asked, wanting as much information as I could get right now.

"I'm not sure, but I think most of the old folks made it back. I was sent here to request support as soon as possible. As for what happened . . ." He looked unsure.

That was good, nobody knowing how badly things had gone was ideal. It would be even more ideal if we could get people out here and get it fixed before anyone from the city found the massive area of distorted space and the crater.

"I suspect a magical phenomenon, perhaps some kind of beast. For the safety of the populace, have the mayor keep them inside the walls, it will be safer that way," I ordered, hoping to get damage control going immediately.

"People won't like it, miss . . . but you're probably right. Will you be returning?"

"I know they won't like it, and not just yet, I've got to put in the proper paperwork here. Don't worry, my guard will keep me safe and these way stations are well-fortified." At my look, he understood and quickly made his way to his mount, hopping up and riding toward the city.

As soon as he was out of earshot I walked up to the nearby worker, who was frantically writing things down. I recognized her as the woman who'd met us when we arrived. She still looked quite unhappy, and very focused on the task at hand.

"Did he give you anything to send off?" I asked.

"A preliminary alert, I'm writing my report now," she answered, not even looking up.

"May I?" I asked, holding my hand out.

The woman looked irritated but obliged, handing over the mayor's letter and letting me have a look at what she was writing. I skimmed them both after breaking the seal on the former and picking up the latter. Both pieces of paper were then rolled together and deposited in the nearby stove.

"Excuse me! Who exactly do you think you are!? When I speak to your superiors . . ." she began to rant but held her tongue when the armored man behind me stepped forward.

"Let me be clear, I am not some official sent here for compliance, the rest you do not need to know. You will exclude the information about what has happened from all of your reports, until told what to put there. As for my superior in this matter, his name is Emperor Durin, you may file whatever complaints you have with him when it is done. For now though, we need to get to the gate immediately, because this situation is far out of hand. Ah, and you need to stay here until told otherwise, there's nothing out there you want to be involved in." My voice was harsher than normal as I spoke, I didn't have time to deal with anyone in my way right now.

She scoffed, and I was sure that she was still thinking she'd have someone to rant to later. It might have been an issue, but right now she turned and led us to the gate room, which was what I needed. If this woman was fool enough to think that approaching one of the many people I'd be bringing for backup about my actions, she'd quickly find out how wrong she was.

The gate room was dark and cool, unbothered by all the goings-on above and around it. Whoever had made these had basically built each like a bunker and buried them, to stave off attack if I had to guess, or contain any mishaps. They also all looked pretty much the same, with a panel for turning the thing on, and a few additional readouts to show mana levels and the like.

With practiced movements, the attendant walked over to the panel and placed a hand on it, activating the magical item. I watched as the mana crept from its storage in the item, flowing over it. There was a brief flash of the gateway coming to life, and then it blinked out again with a loud pop. The failure made my stomach almost fall out of my body. The second and third failures to activate didn't help either, and the worker began to look a bit concerned.

"That's not good, let me take a look," I said, stepping forward.

"Absolutely not! This is a vital, irreplaceable magical relic!" The shouting was once again stopped by Ulanion interspersing himself between us, and moving her firmly to the side.

"If she can't shut up while I work, you're welcome to knock her out or something," I advised as I moved to the panel.

Ulanion sighed. "The difference between knocking someone out and killing them is too slight to even joke about, but I will restrain her if needed."

I assumed he knew his business as I got down to mine, the attendant had already been let in on the fact that I wasn't to be bothered, but some people would always insist on learning the hard way. It might be advisable to see if I could have her transferred when we got back.

The panels that these gates ran on were pretty complex things, not that most people would know that. The readouts and information both the panels and the gate itself had were pretty impressive. Most people wouldn't know or care about that, as the part for standard users was made as simple as it could be, but if you knew how to get into some of the deeper parts you could see more complex readouts. Having built several similar models, and studied this particular one for years, I was privy to those bits of knowledge.

Primarily, the gate was repeating the same information, "Connection Failure." I got to see this notice several more times as the gate briefly flashed without my input.

"What are you doing?!" I was asked loudly from the side.

"That isn't me. The other side realized we attempted to make a gate, and are trying to make one here. They're meeting with the same success we did. This is all standard protocol, have you not read the manual?" The manual in question being the updated user manual for these gates, which Mystien's lab had published, and I knew for a fact distributed to each and every portal location.

After one more quick blink of the gate activating, it stopped. "That was attempt five, which means they will now revert to one attempt at connection establishment once a day, and dispatch a squad to this area to aid us with haste." That too was in the manual.

The many failed connections had let me find the relevant part of the readouts and rune sequences though. This one wasn't immediately obvious to me, as there were a number of issues that could happen. The most likely by our guesses were all pretty easy error codes, but this one was buried, and I needed to consult the sequences written on the gate itself to find the exact problem.

Ulanion looked on with wide eyes at the stream of obscenities I let loose in both the human tongue and Atali. I went on and on, wearing out every curse I knew and even added a few of the more effective English ones.

"That bad?" he asked.

"There's interference and the gateway connection is unstable. They're still seeing each other but have realized that things are so wrong in-between us that they're refusing to keep it open. Safety protocol built-in, and no way to turn it off," I answered.

"Don't suppose you can change the sequence?" he asked hesitantly.

"You cannot alter any item's functions outside of the parameters once it's built, you know this." I sighed. "And this one is not made to be worked around."

"Looks like we're on our own then," he said.

"Looks like."

✦

CHAPTER 35

AID

The way station woman had left us to go and gather the other workers here. There were only six in total, all of which were aware of the gate. For now though, we needed to look at all the assets we had.

"You handled that poorly," Ulanion said.

"Excuse me?" I glared at him, but at his gaze I faltered a bit.

"You made an enemy of that woman when you didn't need to, and now we need her help. You handled it poorly."

I hated to admit he was right, but . . . "She was snippy, and I didn't have time . . ."

"There was plenty of time, Alana, more than enough to remain calm and polite, and let her screw herself if she got in the way." The judgment in his eyes was harsh, and I found myself unable to meet them.

"Crap," I said. "Any advice? This is my first time really in charge of something this big . . ."

"When the others arrive, apologize, then act properly. If she continues being unruly, she will look like the one who's out of line," he said.

I had to sigh. "Okay, sorry for screwing that up."

He leaned over and gave me a kiss on the cheek. "We all make mistakes. Do better, and keep in mind what the people who've let their power go to their head have done to you. Now, they're coming, get ready." His senses weren't as amazing as some people I knew, but they were still way better than mine.

I had enough time to compose myself before the staff filed in, all looking toward us. One of them looking openly hostile while the others looked concerned. I couldn't see an aura on any of them, and my guess was that this place was so far out that there really weren't any mages stationed here at the moment, instead relying on devices and the like.

Taking in a deep breath I began, "Good afternoon, firstly, let me apologize for my short attitude, as things have gone quite wrong in ways no one was properly ready for." I nodded as politely as I could to the woman I'd chewed out. "For the moment, please call me Jenna, though that isn't actually my name. You have not been informed, but my companion and I were sent here to investigate a potential weapon from our enemies. I cannot tell you what, and I cannot tell you why here, but it is a fact that we are now unable to use the gate system here, and there is a large disturbance a few miles outside the town which I cannot fix alone."

There were three men and three women who all read over the authorization papers I passed forward in silence. These were the ones from Durin that told everyone I could basically do what I wanted, and as each looked at them, they were stunned. Things had gone massively awry, and now we needed to come up with a plan.

"How bad is it?" one of the men queried.

"Honestly? I'm not sure, but bad. I don't think there is immediate danger to us, but I cannot confirm that. My main concerns at the moment are reestablishing contact with our superiors and keeping the knowledge of these events contained. Originally, I was planning to secure aid from our forces, but that is no longer on the table, and I'm not sure how long the townsfolk will be willing to stay inside their walls."

"How do we know that you're not some traitor, sent here to take over this place and us?" the erstwhile individual asked.

"Because if I was sent to take over, at this point I would just kill all of you, and being that I'm a fully trained battlemage, and my friend here is quite potent as well, we are more than capable of such," I answered.

"Pfft, nonsense," the woman replied.

There was a slight blur, and Ulanion appeared beside her in a flash. "It is not. We mean you no harm, but we are fully capable of it should we choose." His voice was calm and controlled, and the hand he rested on the woman's shoulder light, but the message was clear.

One of the men spoke now, his green eyes flashing over the papers I'd handed them. He pulled out a small tool that looked like a magnifying glass, which was clearly magical in nature, and moved it over them; that was something I wasn't familiar with. "Clara, you're out of order. This is a very unusual situation, but it's pretty clear this Jenna woman and her guard aren't our enemies. These papers are genuine, at least as far as I can tell anyway, and I've seen plenty of missives over the years."

One of the other women raised her hand carefully before speaking. "Um, even if we do believe you, there's not much we can do here, is there? None of us are casters, and it seems like you might need someone like that to help with . . . whatever went wrong."

I'd been thinking about that, and I could have hugged her for bringing it up.

"I'm a bard, and while alone I might not be able to do much, I've seen this sort of magic before. I propose the group of us go to the scene of the disaster and attempt to repair what happened there using gestalt-type magic. If we're successful, even if it's only a partial success, I'm hoping the gate can be rendered functional again," I explained. "It will involve you seeing some things you'll not be able to share with anyone, but since you're not mages, and not specialists in the field, I think the security risk is minimal. Though you may be reassigned or something afterward."

"I still don't trust them, and I'm not going," Clara declared.

"That's fine, someone would need to stay here to keep an eye on things anyway. While we are away though, I'd advise you to think about the fact that there are only two of us, and our stated goal, and all attempts at action so far, have been to return through this portal back to where we came from. That place is Emperor Durin's, and is swarming with his people, if we weren't here with permission, or were enemies of some kind, that would be suicide." I turned to the others, who nodded with me, though one seemed a bit hesitant. That was about the nicest way I could tell her to shut up, and it did make sense.

"When do we leave?" the green-eyed man asked; he seemed to be the leader of this particular group.

"Right now, if you've got some extra horses, ours are . . . missing."

"Sounds good. Clara, you're on the desk till we get back, but lock everything up. Ed, Connor, kindly go and saddle up horses for us. Jewel, Gail, could you two please grab some basic supplies, a day's worth just in case, please, and some of the swords as well." The people began to move out quickly, all heading to their tasks.

Once they'd all gone, he turned back to me. "I've got a few more questions, if you don't mind," he said as he handed back my paperwork.

"I may not be able to answer them, but I'll try," I said.

"Where exactly are we going, and what are we dealing with?" he asked.

"I could show you on a map, but it's a location a few miles outside the far gate of the city, near one of the lakes . . . There's a crater, and a magical field there that I believe to be the source of our problem. As for danger, we won't be going into the phenomenon, so it should be minimal. By the way, I didn't catch your name."

"Klaus, a pleasure. Anything else?"

There was something I could share. "Hmm, I think the lake there is draining, into the mines is my guess, or some kind of sinkhole. I doubt it's that dangerous, but we should be aware of shifting ground."

He nodded, and we headed out.

The ride to the scene of the disaster was longer than I'd wanted it to be, but that was the way of things. It let me get a better look at the landscape as we approached, and the ongoing mess that was the local water supply being decimated. As we got closer and closer to the scene of the explosion, I saw streams going backwards and ponds draining, some already empty. That was quite a lot of fluid movement, and who knew what it would do to the locals.

It was easy to tell when our help first saw the site, as all of them began to mutter.

"Woah,"

"What in the world . . ."

"But . . . how?"

So far as I could tell, the damage to the local space hadn't grown any, and that was a small mercy. The lake however, was not as we left it. It looked like a draining tub, a small whirlpool at the bottom sucking in everything it could. It also looked like it might not continue for too much longer, as I couldn't see anything else feeding into this area, all the former streams now dry.

"That is certainly something there. What do you need us to do?"

"Okay, what songs do you all know?" I asked.

The list they gave me might as well have been in Greek. I knew none of them, I'd heard of none of them, and I had a pretty good repertoire at this point, all bards did.

"Okay, okay, screw it, I'll teach you one that's pretty easy. I'm going to need you all to sing along with me, or hum or whatever. If you forget the words, that's fine, just keep going. Ready?"

I got a chorus of nods and affirmations.

"Oh, the summer time has come . . ."

CHAPTER 36

✦

SPACE-TIME MAINTENANCE

As the song swelled and my mana became stronger and easier to manipulate, I began trying to wrap it around the massive knot before me. Even with the power, I couldn't encompass all of it though. The tangled mess of space flowed and wavered, spitting out and surging from one moment to the next, invisibly as some internal current pushed and pulled.

Frustrated, I instead looked at one of the parts. It was smaller, bubbling to the edge of the blob that I'd impressed on the world. I reached out again, the mana like water as it wove around the little anomaly, and began to slowly shrink it. This was just one of many, many such bits, and nothing compared to the main body of the beast. At least as it pushed down, it didn't seem to swell back up.

As I tried to cut the cancer in the world out one bit at a time, I began to become convinced that there was something over the larger area. Was this what was causing the gate to have issues? It was subtle and expansive, as large as the crater at least. Should I try to deal with that or the easier-to-spot bits first? I was unsure and, frankly, a bit out of my own depth here.

I began to reflect on my lack of education in something like physics or calculus, or anything even vaguely resembling space back in my own world, and how I couldn't know this would happen. Would it have mattered though? Nobody there could manipulate space like I could, so I kind of doubted they'd have anticipated this result. There was also magic involved, which, no matter how much it resembled what I remembered of physics, clearly wasn't.

With great effort, I managed to prune away three of the little growths before I had to stop. They were all among the smaller side, and even then, wrangling them was both a mentally exhausting and mana-intensive fight. I looked over to the others singing with me, and all but Ulanion looked dog-tired. The process had taken a couple of hours in total, standing out on the open plains.

"You all okay?" I asked.

"Just not used to singing for hours . . ." I looked around and realized that we weren't too far off from nightfall.

"Did it even do anything?" one of my assistants asked slightly hoarsely.

"Yes, though not as much as I'd hoped . . ."

I took one last look at the mess before we all began the process of mounting up.

That night when I finally fell asleep, I dreamed, dreamed about all I'd seen and done over the past day, about the ripples and tangles, about how badly I'd messed up, and about a singular eye, a thousand eyes, and none at all, staring, groping and pulling, turning and twisting in a trillion directions at the frayed edges. Needless to say that I woke up in a cold sweat and couldn't get back to sleep.

The next morning, as we approached the hole once more, armed with a slew of new songs, simple dances, and a drum someone had dug up from the way station's back rooms, I saw something interesting. Deep in the lake bed, the soil was cracking and dry, and in the hole at the crater's bottom was a bright shine.

"What's that?" Klaus asked, eyes flicking down.

"Does it matter?" one of the women asked.

"Maybe. I'd like to see it regardless," he said as he looked at me.

I spun up a small viewing spell, the same one I'd used in the mountains. Nobody was crazy enough to go down there into the massive crater right under an undulating spacial anomaly. It zoomed in enough for us to see that the shine in question was a mix of blackish cubical crystals and a few silvery metal blobs holding them together.

"Miss . . . I hate to impose, but would it be possible to get one of those? It might go a long way to helping with the damage this mission had done . . ." the man asked.

I smiled. "Silver ore?"

"Yes, ma'am, and those bits might be actual silver."

I'd long mastered the spell to pick things up at a distance, and so this wasn't too hard. While he looked closely at the sample-sized bit, I locked my eyes on his. "After we're done, and not before, will you get more? Going down there right now is dangerous, and I've already got more than enough work."

"Sorry, miss, but this could turn the town around," he explained.

"I understand, but that will wait until after we're done."

It was at our first break that the first snake slithered out of the crater, the hole down into the mines and caves below letting it see light. Everyone faltered as it spotted us and became a silver blur. Ulanion met it before it made it all the way to us, the beast's head flying as his sword cut it off.

"Don't stop, we need to get this done," he said.

Over the next hour we saw three, the hour after that, ten. On the third hour, the beasts were emerging almost every other minute and I could tell that our warrior was getting tired. Ulanion focused, sweat dripping down his face. The snakes themselves weren't much of a threat, but there seemed to be no end to them.

"We need to plug that hole," I said, trying not to gag on the smell of blood.

"Tell me you've got something," he replied, killing another as it emerged.

"Nothing permanent, but yeah . . ."

I got Klaus to take up the drum to a simple repeating beat, got the others to dance, and I whistled the theme. Popular TV shows didn't exist in this world, but I needed a bit of cold, so winter was certainly coming today. Bit by bit a crystal of ice formed in the depression, filling the opening into the caves below. The first one failed, falling into the hole, but after that I began building around the opening, slowly working my way inwards as the structure got thicker.

My main hope was that the snakes would be deterred by the cold, since it was well-known that normal ones were rather dissuaded by it. I was also low on options, not having the expertise to do anything with the mud or dirt, and already tired. Ulanion had the good sense to throw the corpses on top of the growing plug, which would surely help with the smell. After a good couple inches or so of solid ice was piled over the sinkhole, I finally stopped.

"Won't last forever," one of the girls observed. "Can we put dirt or something over it?"

"Maybe, or sawdust," I said, remembering one of those history lessons about warships from WWII. "We can add sawdust to make it last longer, but that's unlikely. The town might have hay or something, that might work . . . we can get some, tell them our horses are running low." I wasn't sure how much I was having to lie as of late, it'd been fun at first, but it wore on me.

I didn't know, I was too beat. I could cast a lot, and I could cast a lot more and a lot better with a gestalt like this, but there were limits. I was running on fumes already, unable to keep up with the demands. The only good news was that the disaster hanging above our little snake hole had visibly shrunk with our efforts today.

After another spree of attacking the anomaly, I had to stop. I was getting better at this, of course, casting the same spell over and over did improve things, but it was still draining.

"Are you okay? You look terrible," one of the girls—Jewel—said as she came over and placed an arm around me.

"I'm out. Any more mana and I might collapse. We need to rest and start again tomorrow, or maybe try the gate, I don't know."

After a good night's sleep, we gathered up a cart at the way station and made our way out toward Silversprings. I was the only one of the girls going, the others having been judged to be too odd. My own inclusion was justified by the fact that my guard wouldn't be able to go without me, and I needed to consult with the mayor anyway. It was a poor excuse, but an excuse nonetheless.

Before we even got there, I heard the bells, bells declaring emergency, bells calling for all people to aid or hide.

Durin's Fortress

A frantic knocking came at my door, answered quickly by one of the guards on duty. The man looked elated, waving a piece of paper in his hand.

"My Emperor, good news, we've reestablished contact with two of the gates. They report no casualties," he said as soon as he'd been acknowledged.

"Swilstown and Red Rock?" I asked.

"I . . . yes, that's correct." He looked at me like I was some kind of genius.

I wasn't, the simple fact was, that of the twelve gates we'd lost contact with, those were the furthest from Silversprings. I walked back over to my map and looked at it once more, removing the pins marking the disabled gates. At the very least I knew that girl had found something.

CHAPTER 37

✦

SILVERSPRINGS MELEE

The bells sounded harsh and clear through the morning light as our party sped toward the gate. Something was wrong, something was so, so very wrong, and I had an idea what. The only thing holding us back was the cart, which could get a good bit of speed but was limited by design; too much speed and it'd come apart.

As we got to the gate, I could see the lone guard in a panic. He was looking everywhere as his hand white-knuckled his spear. When he saw us coming, he looked like we'd been sent straight on to save him, recognition dawning on his face. With a quick motion the gate sped open due to an emergency mechanism he'd used to let us in as quickly as possible. Soon as we were through, another motion slammed it shut.

"Situation?" Ulanion yelled up at him.

"Attack, bell pattern signal means monsters!" he returned. It wasn't uncommon for a city to have a certain way to ring their bells for various emergencies.

"And you're not going to go help!?" Jewel screamed hysterically.

"Ignore her," I added. "Standard procedure to guard all entrances during attack, good job following." The girl glared at me but said nothing else.

The guardsman had clenched his teeth for only a moment. "Right, the ladies can shelter in the guardhouse here, but I see you gentlemen have weapons, mind going to aid?" he asked.

"I'm going," I said without explanation, and jumped from the cart over toward Ulanion's horse. The beast nearly jumped, but he managed to control it while plucking me from the air and settling me on the saddle in front of him. The guard looked surprised, but just nodded while the two other girls in our party headed for the large iron door by the gate.

Ulanion and I, as well as the three men from the way station, rode with haste toward the far side of the city. The streets were clear and empty, and the only people I saw were those glancing furtively out of windows at our passing. Klaus, Ed, and Connor were all behind the horse I was on, having seen what the Elven man could do, and serving as backup as we streaked over the cobbles.

Finding the emergency was the easiest thing in the world. Right in front of the far gate the melee was on. Ten or so defenders stood, along with the town's two bards against nearly twice that number of beasts. Other men had gotten in on the fighting as well, and nearly a dozen were encircled by the battle line in various stages of injury. A few of the defenders had clearly fallen to the onslaught, dead eyes looking skyward.

The townsfolk were, for their part, giving an excellent showing, having killed a large number of the beasts, and as we came near I saw how. Several of the monsters darted forward, only for the mother of the caster pair to unleash a scream at them. It was the most basic of all bardic combat magic, but more than enough to disorient and stun the boa-sized snakes, who were then dispatched by guards that darted forwards.

I added my own scream as I reached down to grab the reins and Ulanion leapt from our mount. While it wasn't really the time for it, I couldn't help but feel a swell of joy at how much larger my area of effect was, or how much the silver monstrosities squirmed in pain rather than just being stunned.

Ulanion landed silently like a cat, having drawn his sword midair. He pounced forward and into the beasts, leaving a trail of severed heads and bodies as he passed. To a normal soldier these things were threats, but they were hardly much compared to most magical beasts; the main issue for us would be their numbers.

Our arrival ended the fight. Not only were we backup the beleaguered defenders desperately needed; we had what was needed to slay these monsters. The mother-son caster pair from this city wasn't trained for combat, and the soldiers likewise for magical beasts. They were mostly here for peacekeeping with the occasional drunken brawl or small infestation, not this. The soldiers of the city likely had little, if any, real training beyond basic weapons and law. Not so with our group; both Ulanion and I were old hands at killing things that needed to die, and all of the way station employees were given some combat training, just in case.

We also lucked out that the large amount of blood on the ground seemed to be attracting the silver snakes. If they'd spread throughout the city, dealing with them would have been nigh impossible. With each body on the pile, more and more of them came, a feeding frenzy. Until they stopped, their numbers depleted as the last few fell, not even trying to flee, but still attempting to get in and attack us.

Everyone was exhausted by the end of it though, several bending over to gasp and pant while others still looked on edge, eyes scanning for more enemies. I didn't hesitate to move forward to help the injured, some of which were bleeding quite badly. There were more varied wounds than I'd expected, with bites and cuts, along with some who'd just been hit by the speeding monster's body and had bones broken by a whipping tail or whatnot.

"Are these things poisonous?" I asked Sloane.

"Venomous," he ejected before inhaling to continue.

"Venom is a poison, jackass, now answer the question." I was not in the mood for grammar lessons from the local himbo.

"Yes, but not enough to worry about. We should focus on the other injuries first," his mother helpfully told me from the side.

"Thank you."

In the end, there were five dead, eight injured enough that we only stabilized them, and over a dozen with less critical wounds. Nobody was trained in triage, and while there were three healers, it just wasn't enough. I got looks when I passed over a man coughing blood to treat two who were bleeding badly but could be definitely saved, and it felt horrible like it always would. They didn't question it though, only looking on with narrowed eyes as I went about my work.

The mayor saw me but waited until I finished with the healing before asking for a word.

"You're a caster," he said after we returned to his home.

He'd been at the melee, along with one of his sons. Their mail armor was old and slightly rusted but among the only pieces in the town, and their swords more like parade weapons of display pieces than blades meant for battle, but they'd been here, and that counted for a lot.

"I am," I answered.

"You didn't tell me, you said you weren't a noble . . ."

"I did not, and I am not a noble."

"You've been out of the town for days, keeping your secrets and consulting none. I need to know, did you have a hand in this disaster? I need to know what happened." He was on edge, clearly not ready for this kind of situation.

"I did, though this result was not anticipated in the extreme. As for what happened, I'm afraid I cannot tell you, and can only ask that you extend your trust further." I tried to keep myself calm, but truth be told, we were all out of our depth.

"My people are dead, and others might well join them by nightfall, and you want me to trust you!? None of this has happened before, not like this, and you want me to just act as if it's of no issue? I thought the empire was different, I thought you cared about the people, and now this!" His hand thrust forward to grab at my shirt.

Physical magic users were so fast it was like they didn't move sometimes. Ulanion wasn't as strong as my father, and I suspected even my brother would outperform him in many ways, but he was no slouch. Before the formerly controlled mayor could touch me, the man found himself slammed against a nearby wall, the plaster cracking where he struck.

"I understand you are angry, and in pain. I understand you need an outlet for it, Mallowsweet, but we are not your enemies, and I will not permit you to put hands on her. Am I understood?" Ulanion's voice was firm but calm, making it clear that he bore the man no real ill will.

"The empire is different," I said. "You and your people were never disposable, and never supposed to be in this mess. When things went wrong, I did what I could to keep you away from it all, away from the danger while we worked to set it right. Because there are things out there you don't need to be involved with, that could bring ruin onto your town. We didn't abandon you, we did what we could to protect you."

"You expect me to believe that! I saw you turn away while Jacob drowned in his own blood!" He must have known the man from earlier, and known him well.

"When time and resources are limited, you have to focus on those who will die but can absolutely be saved. It's . . . never good, but it saves the most lives in the worst situations," I answered, and I could see the pain on his face. He knew it was the truth, but it was easy to blame me for all that had happened, and he was not totally wrong. "For what it is worth, I am sorry."

"As if that changes anything at all! Very well, do what you will, you've already made it abundantly clear that you can. Though if there is any decency in you, you'll leave me and mine out of it." Ulanion let him stalk out after that.

As he slammed the door, I sank into a nearby chair and buried my face in my hands. How had things gone so wrong?

CHAPTER 38

✦

NEAR MISS

I spent the rest of the day feeling dejected. We were given all the supplies we needed. More than enough to plug up the hole in the lake. My mouth tasted like ash as we headed out of the town. Some of the members thanked us, others gave suspicious looks—particularly those closest to the mayor.

This was my fault. My actions had caused the damage that was keeping reinforcements away and causing these monsters to go wild.

Rather than head back to the way station, we made our way toward the mines. My first job would be to collapse them. It was the least I could do. I felt terrible about not even considering that it might cause a mass of monsters to escape and rampage. But I genuinely hadn't.

Over the next several days I would wake up, check the mines for new exits, refreeze the cap on the lake bed, cut away as much of the cancerous spatial distortion as possible, then start all over again. Bit by bit it shrank, the gaping maw of disaster slowly closing. It also got easier, that was the thing about repeating the same spell over and over again.

As for the silver snakes, there were more attacks, but they were getting few and far between. The creatures didn't like being above ground, and they hadn't all spilled out of their caves, so there were just the few that managed to wriggle out of the imperfect defenses and those who'd already gotten out but hadn't come to the city. They also found the horses Ulanion and I had lost before we did, and it turned out the snakes could rip pieces of flesh off—the results would inspire nightmares for weeks.

Six days after the initial disaster, we saw the line approaching before we left in the morning. Soldiers spread across the plain in a wave, only two deep as their chargers carried them forward, lances raised.

The way station staff looked as if they were about to cry. Klaus quickly organized them to get the flags up in the proper code to display that we were both secure and friendly. I hadn't thought about that, but he was quite right, it wouldn't do to have them think we were invaders.

I felt even more vindicated as the group drew in, At the center of the group were six blazing auras. Five were clearly physical magic users, arranged to rip through any and all who might stand in their way, while the final one was a wizard, hanging back just enough to watch over everything and provide ranged support. In the center of the formation was a short figure whose armor, aura, and carriage I would recognize anywhere, helmet or not.

"Glen? Is that you?" I asked as they approached. It had been a while since I'd seen him, but he was still the same short man of iron he'd always been.

I'd known him for years, at least in passing. We'd met as part of a school project, and run into each other every now and then since, even going together to the Elven lands. He was an unmovable rock in a fight and was able to survive attacks that would cripple lesser men without a scratch.

The line had slowed, seeming to understand from our stances that we weren't their enemy. The man I'd addressed took a moment to respond, clearly looking me over.

"Why is it that every time there's some disaster you seem to be involved?" he said.

I scoffed, certainly it wasn't *every* time . . . then I heard laughter from beside me.

"I've been wondering the same thing," said Ulanion. Traitor.

"I do not . . . well . . . not every time." My halting attempt at rebuff got chuckles from both.

"So, based on my orders, I'm guessing something's gone horribly wrong and fixing it is probably going to hurt. Mind filling me in where you can?"

"How much do your men know?" I asked, hopeful.

"They've gotten approval, though keep specifics out of it."

"Right . . . magical disaster due to my personal work is interfering with the gate network as far as I can tell. We've been cleaning up where we can, but it's slow going. The interaction also released a number of minor beasts onto the countryside who've been assaulting the city, after draining the nearby lakes. Danger is probably minimal, but we'll need to keep an eye out. If you and yours are willing, we might be able to clean up the last remnants." That was about as nonspecific of an explanation they could get.

"The snakes, right? We ran into some this morning. What's the damage from those?" It seemed they had a reason for their war footing in their approach.

"A few casualties in the city, but otherwise minor." I thought for a moment before adding, "But there's some evidence that we may have found a new section of the mine that could help the town overall."

I felt terrible that those people had to die, but the work had to be done, and the result was not expected by anyone. The mayor had every right to be angry, but there wouldn't be any real blame assigned to the deaths of his people.

"The city is well then? We'll need to check on them," he said.

"The mayor is . . . understandably unhappy with the governance right now. He wasn't filled in and feels betrayed, but I don't think he'll rebel or anything, if that's what you're asking; I think he mostly blames me."

"There first, then afterward we'll see what we can do about the monster problem."

As one, we made our way to Silversprings, there was a town meeting called, and I got a chance to see everyone there. I could say that at best our reception was mixed. There were a few people who were clearly containing their hostility, and others who weren't bothering, roughly half if I had to guess felt that we'd burned them, though were wise enough not to say anything about it. Glen gave a small speech, he'd not been much for words in any of our last meetings, but seemed capable of at least that much now. I wondered if he'd gone through a lot of training to now lead this group of soldiers.

When we arrived at the site of the detonation, the soldiers looked shocked. Their mage really understood though—it was easy to tell because I could have shoved my whole fist in his mouth as it gaped, his hand nervously running through his short hair.

"That's . . . something," Glen said as he looked at the distortion.

"How . . . how big was the explosion," the mage asked.

"Big enough, and we need to fix it," I answered. I wasn't exactly sure how to quantify the blast, but it was surely significant.

"Agreed, what do you need us to do?"

We all set up around the crater, and unlike the way station employees, these men knew some songs I did. As one, we all began one of the empire's standard marching numbers. A few of the soldiers had instruments of their own, to keep time for such things and convey orders. There were a hundred in all, nearly twice what I could normally utilize for a gestalt, but having extras on hand wouldn't hurt.

I began the spell, much as I had before, but gestalt was something else. On my own, the magic flowed, but the more I added, the stronger it worked. With a small group, it was like leading a troupe, but with a large one, it was like being a conductor before an orchestra. It served much the same, but it was quite a rush to feel that much power responding all at once.

My magic worked on instinct, wrapping around the knot and beginning to chew away at it. I could feel it, smoothing and pulling here and there, setting everything back to how they should be. I could also feel the mess I'd made, and all around it, like looking at it with all of my senses enhanced, it was nearly physical.

As I unmade the distortion, it began to release things. The first of which was the air and water tied up in it, along with a few stones. They didn't speed out, but rather fell to the crater below. This wasn't like the explosion. Then there was something else.

The world almost seemed to groan as I felt . . . attention. This wasn't anger, or irritation, nor pleasure, nor hatred, nor any other emotion that made any sense. No, it was just the feeling of being . . . noticed, in passing. It was like someone seeing a speck of dust on their glasses while reading a book, only foreign, strange, indescribable. This magic was making big waves in local space and something, somewhere, saw them.

Some of the soldiers faltered in their song, the better trained ones kept singing as reflex, and I heard Glen's voice in a corner of my mind yelling at them not to stop. Could they feel what I did? I doubted it. I was at the center of this. There were two options: I could either keep the spell going, keep trying to untangle the distortion and hope that without it we'd be hidden, or I could drop it like a flaming poker, hoping the magic faded before we attracted any more attention, for I felt that we'd not survive it if whatever that was looked on us fully.

It wasn't here, wasn't in this world, but this world was moving, and moving things attracted eyes. We needed to stop moving, and look as if we never had—there was only one option. I swept up all of the unused soldiers into my spell, grabbing all of their songs. It was too much, I knew it was too much, but this distortion needed to go and now. The magic, which I'd been moving like a conductor, fought, it was frantic, the sweet music of it replaced by noise. It didn't matter, it wasn't important, I needed it to obey, and so I pointed the discordant spell where it needed to go and held on for the ride.

I pushed and slammed the spell into place, ramming it down even as the backlash from such an action sent waves of pain through my body. My heart was pounding like a hummingbird's wings as it took hold, lashing deep and causing a brief blast of air and dust as the little hovering bit of twisted space returned to its normal, curved self.

The pressure of observation left, and I fell to my knees, spewing my stomach's contents all over the ground.

The Entity

In a place where time was meaningless unless someone really cared to ask it how it was doing, and space was more like a polite suggestion, a being who was both unfathomably ancient and yet could not have been said to be properly born yet, almost noticed something. It could have flicked at the little passing thing that was on one of its many baubles if it bothered to look, but one of the other ones was doing things that were so very much more interesting.

CHAPTER 39

✦

RETURN

Ulanion

Our group fled back to the city. Whatever that thing had been was gone, and now we could return home. The fortress would be our destination, but getting back to the city was our first concern. I looked down at the reason for that in my arms, her hair wild in the wind.

Something happened during the spell. We all felt it, the feeling of approaching, unstoppable doom. That feeling had grown like a massive shadow on the world until, with a final pop, the crater suddenly went back to normal—or as normal as a massive hole in the ground could look. At that point, the woman I was now racing along with had fallen over, vomited violently, and then fainted, mumbling. Blood leaked from her nose, her ears, her eyes, and the corners of her mouth—clearly the spell had gone horribly wrong.

My mount was pushing as hard as it could. A few men lingered behind to keep an eye on things while the rest of us went to get medical help. The pair in the town might not be able to do much, but they could at least try to stabilize her.

The gates grew closer, and seeing our charge the guards quickly moved out of the way. I'd only seen where the bards lived on some of the maps, but my memory was pretty good and I was sure we could find them.

Glen pulled up beside me once we were within the walls. I had to slow down a little, if only to navigate and take corners safely.

"Calm down, haste here could make things worse," he advised.

"I disagree. There are a pair of casters in town, they might be able to help. Can you send one of your men to the way station to check on things?" I replied as we made our way to the northern part of the town.

He turned and barked a series of commands to some men, and a troop of three broke off from our mass. A few civilians ducked out of the road, pulling children to the side and out of our way.

It was fortunate that finding my target was easy. I knew the general area and just had to look for the only place around with trees. They were small, and it looked like they were pruned often, but the little copse was exactly where I expected. The house was on the nicer side, and the plants near the door were flowering brilliantly, a few crimson apples hung from the branches there.

I climbed down from my mount and quickly hauled Alana over to the door. I banged on it hard, perhaps too hard as there was a light cracking noise the third time my fist connected. The son we'd fought with appeared at the door, looking aggrieved.

"What in the world . . . oh goodness." His eyes grew in size as he took in the woman in my arms. "Oh, shit, get inside."

I was directed to a couch where I could set Alana down. "I'm not sure what happened, she was casting, and when the spell ended she puked and then this."

The man paid me little mind, turning and yelling "MOTHER! FRONT ROOM!" And while his voice wasn't too loud, the house still shook with magic. I had little doubt she could hear it.

"Can you help her?" I asked as he looked over her wounds.

"I don't know, I've never seen this kind of injury before," he replied before he began whistling.

His mother arrived and began her own appraisal of the situation. She must have heard her son, because she asked, "Was she casting? How many in the gestalt?" My look must have told her all she needed. "Too many. She'll need a proper priest, and we don't have one."

"Can you help us move her? If you do that it'll be enough."

The woman nodded and turned back, adding her voice to her son's performance.

I found a comfortable place nearby and set to watching. Nothing happened for a while. The two bards worked their magic over our own injured caster. They went slow, but I could tell it was having an effect. Some of the color returned to her face, and the bleeding stopped.

I heard the horses before I saw anything, and turned to answer the door. I didn't want our hosts to stop working until we were ready. Outside

came the knights who'd been sent to the way station, along with the mayor.
I could only assume that they'd needed directions, and he didn't look particularly happy.

"Status?" Glen asked from beside me.

"Good, sir," the leading horseman replied. It was the best news I could
imagine.

"May I ask what's happening?" Mayor Mallowsweet chimed in, his
eyes half closed.

"Miss Jenna was badly injured and needs to be evacuated," I said.

"How unfortunate," he replied with dripping sarcasm.

In the split second he had to reflect on things, he must have realized
his mistake. I'd tolerated his actions for a while now, it was understand-
able, his people had been hurt and died because of our mistake, but there
was a limit. My fist clenched and I stepped forward, only to find the leading knight's hand tight on my arm. He was slower than I was, but also
stronger. I turned toward him, ready for a fight, until I saw his own angry
eyes.

"You were the mayor, correct?" he asked, and I didn't miss the tense.

"Yes, I am." The man still eyed me, and I wondered if he knew how
close he'd come to me turning his jaw into paste.

"Ah, then I have good news. Your replacement will be here in a few
days, please vacate the mayoral residence with your family." His tone was
calm and cool, even if his eyes told a different story.

After the man had left, I turned to the other knight. "Can you actually
do that?"

"Officially? No, but I'm betting that between myself and your complaints, we can have him removed before anyone can call that bluff. I also
don't want you to kill him, it'd only cause more problems."

Was it an abuse of power? Yes, yes it was. Was it wrong? Also, yes. Was
I still going to do it to punish someone who'd been so flippant about the
woman I was courting almost dying? Why yes, I would indeed.

Alana

I gasped as consciousness returned to me. My whole body felt like it had
been put in a blender and then simmered over a low heat. The groan of
pain must have attracted attention because as soon as I tried to sit up, a
firm hand pushed me back into . . . a bed?

"Shh, it's okay, don't try to get up." I raised my eyes to the speaker, an older man whom I didn't know. He had a medallion around his neck indicating he was a priest of the Shield.

"Ow . . ." I replied with great wisdom.

"It's okay, can you tell me what you remember?"

"There was, it was, had to hide the mess. It was turning toward us!" As I remembered my last moments before passing out, I knelt over the railing and dry heaved, an apt reenactment of that time.

"Calm, calm, you're safe, you're safe, I promise."

I spent most of the rest of the day with the priest and a couple of his compatriots looking over me while I shook like a leaf. It felt as if I'd walked up on a nuke that had not gone off due to a failure to activate, right in front of my house. The pressure of observation was gone, though, and as I sat there thinking I convinced myself that whatever was happening wouldn't happen again so long as we didn't repeat an experiment like that. I still didn't manage to sleep until the priests did something to knock me out.

When I awoke, I had a few visitors. Ulanion had strong-armed his way to my side, and that was nice. Mother came by later as well. The final visitor came with an entourage, though he asked for privacy, and we received it.

"I'm glad you're well," Emperor Durin said. Since we were at his fortress, he'd probably been nearby. "Some of your reports were handed over to me, and I've taken a few actions, but I'd like to hear your thoughts personally, as well, if you don't mind."

It was weird for the ruler of a country to so easily come to see me in the hospital, but I was glad because I had some major thoughts that hadn't yet been written down.

"Shutting down all the gates is my suggestion, and not building any more. Also, we need to find those that idiot princeling got and obliterate them."

"That . . . is an extreme answer, and not going to happen. They're still our strongest strategic resource," he said, surprised.

"Then please keep them well away from each other, if you can. That last test went wrong, more wrong than I could have imagined, and I think we had a near miss on losing that entire region. If that had happened in a city, we'd have thousands dead from the initial detonation alone, and I'd wager it would get worse if there were more gates nearby," I explained.

"I'll take that under advisement. Clearly, you've been through a lot, Alana, and the priests have told me you overdrew on a gestalt, you're lucky to be alive."

He was right on that. I had felt that I was pulling too much, and every bard knew that could be extremely fatal, instinctively when they tried as well. Not that I regretted it at all.

"Please listen to me on this, if you listen to nothing else, please, on this. When I'm back up I'll redesign some wards, and maybe something to clean up around the gates, but they're dangerous. There was . . . something, something out there that could notice us, and I don't think we want that to happen."

"Of course, of course, but for now, rest." He patted my hand gently, and I knew he was just talking. That was no good, but there wasn't much I could do about it. If I kept on, he might even decide that I'd gone crazy, and then I'd lose all access, access I'd need if I wanted to change things in the future.

/ CHAPTER 40

◆

HOME

It took days to get back up and running properly. The priests they brought in assured me I'd recover in time, but also encouraged me to hold off on casting anything for at least the next week. That was annoying. I'd become accustomed the little perks being a caster afforded me, such as floating books over and cleaning stuff, at least when things weren't too hectic.

That, of course, meant that I could go home to rest. As far as we could tell, there was nobody in Lithere after me, and Ulanion would get a chance to go back to his actual duties. It was fortunate that he lived so close. Now we could go out whenever we wanted. Sadly, there were still other people in town who were slightly less easy to deal with.

Mother wasted no chance asking me when I would be marrying my boyfriend, or to imply that my brother was at least trying to be honest. She also somehow found a way to drag me to every function she could. The only ways I could get out of it were either work, which I was on light duty for, or seeing the aforementioned boyfriend. Otherwise I was supposed to be resting and avoiding too much magic.

"I know I've been saying it a lot, but I have to get away from home, it's just too much," I complained to Ulanion at breakfast. I left out that I wanted a private workspace where I could try to figure out spells I'd be hesitant to let anyone else see, and items that could stop the looming disaster of portal proliferation.

"I would invite you to stay with me, but seeing as my room at the barracks is rather small, that would be difficult." Ulanion brushed his hand over my cheek.

"I wish I had a room or something," I said, pouting. It was childish, I knew, but hard to resist.

"Why don't you rent one? Or buy a house or something?" he suggested. "Surely you make enough to afford it."

I nearly dropped my fork. I'd been so used to living with family, or traveling, that it hadn't even occurred to me to just buy a place to live. There were some other things implied in that statement, though, that I hadn't really paid attention to.

"I . . . think I do."

"What do you mean you think you do? You've got savings, right? You've been working for the country for years."

"I guess . . ." I hesitated.

Ulanion slowly put down his silverware. "Alana, what do you do with your wages? You save them, right? I know you know how to run a budget; I've seen you do it. Recently, in fact."

"I mean . . . I mostly just have them sent to my section of the family vault and then get money out as I need it . . . it's not like I spend all that much . . ." I was already having flashbacks to my childhood, of a particular woman who'd lived with me for a while. I could hear her screaming about responsibility already.

I really had little in the way of expenses. I made most of my food myself, or it came from the house kitchens, I didn't spend much on frivolities, and I couldn't stop my mother from making or buying me clothing a few times a year. I probably did have a good amount put away, but I'd never bothered to look.

Ulanion looked divided. "I would tell you off for not thinking about that kind of thing, but seeing as I spent most of my years as a mercenary bouncing from place to place, I'm not sure I have much in the way of a place to stand."

"Right, right, I'll . . . take care of it tonight. Thanks, by the way."

He just shook his head slightly.

It turned out that government work actually paid pretty well at certain levels. I was a caster, and a fairly in-demand and specialized one. That alone meant that I made a very large salary. Plus I was heavily involved in high-level projects that were often covered in a mix of hazard and away-from-home pay. Basically, I had a literal pile of gold. The ledger for my monthly earnings nearly made my eyes bulge. I was earning only slightly less than my father, and he was a general.

That was how three weeks later I ended up standing in the home I'd just purchased. There still weren't proper nobles, and if there had been, this would have been a generational home for my own family. It was near my parents' place, and significantly smaller, the kind of thing one of the noninheriting children would have gotten from the main family. All that suited me well since I liked to travel and didn't need anything insanely huge. My main concern was the large wine cellar, which I was already working on plans to convert.

"It's enormous," Ulanion said as I showed him around. That was true enough, as while it wasn't a proper mansion, it was still quite a big house.

"It has all the things I want, and even has some wards installed, though I'll be adding to those later. Suppose I'll need to hire a staff though, hmm." My parents had insisted on getting something at least this big, if only because of the safety of the area and inbuilt protections—at least they helped me find a place. I suspected they'd also led me here in particular, since it was right next to their house.

"I'm surprised something like this was on the market," he said.

"Almost nobody can afford them, the old nobility had centuries' worth of wealth built up, but now . . . most of these are situated around the old proper estates, and those who could afford them are off-put by the remaining members of the old guard hovering around."

"Makes sense, I guess. What's this room?" he asked politely as we came to a set of double doors, me leading him around by the arm.

"Oh, this?" I smirked. "This is my room."

"Oh, I see . . ." I didn't give him time to finish before pulling him inside. I had a particular housewarming activity that I was most interested in finally getting around to.

Lief, Location Unknown

My men and I sat around the large table. Reports had just come in. *Full success.* We would be ready when the time came to strike. If we had done things properly, they wouldn't even know we were coming.

We were all rough. The war had hardened us from soft nobles into the beaten but unbroken rebellion we now were.

"My friends, and I mean that, for you are all truly my greatest companions. You, each and every one, have stood side by side as our men fell, and disloyal traitors knelt to that conquering bastard. You are the ones who shall ride with me to victory. Our plans are in motion. We merely await the right time. The time when we'll surge forth and destroy the shadows, and bring the light back to our lands." I raised my goblet. "To the light! To the end of the darkness!"

"To the end of the darkness!" they all cheered, raising their glasses.

ABOUT THE AUTHOR

Wandering Agent is the North Carolina–based author of the Melody of Mana series as well as other fantasy and isekai stories.